"Give me [...]," the Executioner said.

"Give me my final release. It is the only thing I ask."

"What is the code?"

"Give me your word. What is on that flash drive is time sensitive. Open it in time and you'll have an intelligence coup that could save lives, perhaps as many lives as I've destroyed in my hubris. Take too long and the window closes."

"How do you know I'll keep my word once you give me the code?" Bolan countered.

"Faith is all I have left. Give me your word and I'll give you the code."

Bolan looked at the former analyst. The man looked back at him. Tears made his eyes look weak and shiny in the unforgiving brightness of the lamp. His head shook with his suppressed emotion.

"Please," the man whispered.

The Executioner looked at the traitor. He nodded once.

MACK BOLAN ®
The Executioner

The Executioner®

Don Pendleton's

COLLISION COURSE

A GOLD EAGLE BOOK FROM

W☉RLDWIDE®

TORONTO • NEW YORK • LONDON
AMSTERDAM • PARIS • SYDNEY • HAMBURG
STOCKHOLM • ATHENS • TOKYO • MILAN
MADRID • WARSAW • BUDAPEST • AUCKLAND

If you purchased this book without a cover you should be aware
that this book is stolen property. It was reported as "unsold and
destroyed" to the publisher, and neither the author nor the
publisher has received any payment for this "stripped book."

Recycling programs
for this product may
not exist in your area.

First edition April 2009

ISBN-13: 978-0-373-64365-3
ISBN-10: 0-373-64365-9

Special thanks and acknowledgment to
Nathan Meyer for his contribution to this work.

COLLISION COURSE

Copyright © 2009 by Worldwide Library.

All rights reserved. Except for use in any review, the
reproduction or utilization of this work in whole or in part
in any form by any electronic, mechanical or other means,
now known or hereafter invented, including xerography,
photocopying and recording, or in any information storage
or retrieval system, is forbidden without the written permission
of the publisher, Worldwide Library, 225 Duncan Mill Road,
Don Mills, Ontario, Canada M3B 3K9.

This is a work of fiction. Names, characters, places and incidents are
either the product of the author's imagination or are used fictitiously,
and any resemblance to actual persons, living or dead, business
establishments, events or locales is entirely coincidental.

® and TM are trademarks of the publisher. Trademarks indicated
with ® are registered in the United States Patent and Trademark
Office, the Canadian Trade Marks Office and in other countries.

Printed in U.S.A.

I have often laughed at the weaklings who thought themselves good because they had no claws.
—Friedrich Nietzsche
1844–1900

The good must have claws—for the battle of good against evil is always fought tooth and nail.
—Mack Bolan

THE
MACK BOLAN
LEGEND

Nothing less than a war could have fashioned the destiny of the man called Mack Bolan. Bolan earned the Executioner title in the jungle hell of Vietnam.

But this soldier also wore another name—Sergeant Mercy. He was so tagged because of the compassion he showed to wounded comrades-in-arms and Vietnamese civilians.

Mack Bolan's second tour of duty ended prematurely when he was given emergency leave to return home and bury his family, victims of the Mob. Then he declared a one-man war against the Mafia.

He confronted the Families head-on from coast to coast, and soon a hope of victory began to appear. But Bolan had broken society's every rule. That same society started gunning for this elusive warrior—to no avail.

So Bolan was offered amnesty to work within the system against terrorism. This time, as an employee of Uncle Sam, Bolan became Colonel John Phoenix. With a command center at Stony Man Farm in Virginia, he and his new allies—Able Team and Phoenix Force—waged relentless war on a new adversary: the KGB.

But when his one true love, April Rose, died at the hands of the Soviet terror machine, Bolan severed all ties with Establishment authority.

Now, after a lengthy lone-wolf struggle and much soul-searching, the Executioner has agreed to enter an "arm's-length" alliance with his government once more, reserving the right to pursue personal missions in his Everlasting War.

1

Mack Bolan had parked in the shadows under the New Jersey freeway overpass. The low-slung black Honda Prelude had heavily tinted windows and boasted a nitrous-augmented engine. Inside the vehicle the Executioner waited, a cell phone and a silenced Beretta 93-R machine pistol on the seat beside him.

The parking lot was hidden from the major urban arterial by an abandoned factory, its windows broken and graffiti covering its walls in a dozen hues of paint. A sour wind, smelling strongly of the ocean, pushed garbage around the vacant lot.

A scrawny one-eyed dog emerged from the mouth of a secondary alley and trotted across the broken asphalt. It nosed around a refuse pile, then lifted its leg against an overturned garbage can.

Bolan shifted inside the car and the dog's head came up, the animal wary and feral. It growled low in its throat, then lazily trotted back toward the safety of the alley it had emerged from.

Ten minutes later a silver TrailBlazer with government plates rolled out of the same alley through the chain-link fence and came to a stop beside the Prelude, nose pointed in the opposite direction.

The driver's window on each car powered down smoothly, and Bolan nodded to the man his old friend Hal Brognola had sent to meet him. The guy was big, with a shaved head and a bristling goatee. Despite the leathers he was wearing, something about the cool appraisal the man gave Bolan screamed "Cop."

"I'm Danson," he said in a gravelly voice. "A friend of mine told me to come see you. Said helping you would clean the slate between us. Since I owe the son of a bitch from way back, I came and brought what he asked."

"What do you have?" Bolan prompted.

Danson lifted a manila envelope from the seat beside him. As he handed it through the open window, Bolan could see the word Hate had been tattooed across the scarred knuckles of the man's big fist.

The envelope wasn't very heavy, and Bolan quickly opened the flap to check its contents.

"Robert Scone. Goes by the street name Sideways. Biker thug. Did a stretch in Attica a couple years ago for aggravated assault on his old lady, a dancer named Shayla. Did a pretty good number on her and got three years," Danson stated.

Bolan grunted and gently shook the contents of the envelope out into his lap. There was a stack of photocopied sheets held together by a paper clip, a police rap sheet from the City of Newark and a blowup of an official mug shot. There was also a pint plastic bowl with a sealed lid. When Bolan held it up he saw the pink of ground hamburger and two horse pills filled with white powder. He looked at Danson.

"Read on," Danson said. "You'll figure it out. Anyway, Sideways was connected to the Outlaws motorcycle gang as a prospect member when he went into Attica. Inside he made his bones against the Black Gangsta Disciples. Typical swastika-wearing bullshit."

Bolan placed the plastic container beside his Beretta and held up the mug shot picture. He let his gaze roam across the photograph, memorizing every detail. His eyes flicked to the information typed beneath the snapshot. Sideways was a big man, six-five and 260 pounds at the time of incarceration. His priors included a DUI, simple assault, several counts of possession of a controlled substance and domestic violence.

"After he made his bones," Danson continued, "he got serious about his career as a criminal. When he got out, he freelanced as muscle for a couple of the Jersey syndicates, arson for hire, collections, extortion, that sort of thing."

Bolan nodded and slid the picture to the bottom of the pile of paperwork he held. He scanned down the page until he found the annotation for Scone's current address. He memorized it.

"The organized-crime squad put some of their confidential informants in his path and started hearing that Sideways was making a rep for himself as a real gunslinger, hijacking freight trucks and teamsters coming out of the Newark airport."

"They nab him?" Bolan asked.

"Yes and no. A cigarette truck on its way into the city gets nabbed. The Newark police finger our man Sideways and do a takedown on the address I just gave you there."

"He was holding?"

"No. No cigarettes, nothing to connect him to the heist. Still, it looks like they got him on a parole violation because the team found some crystal meth and a handgun in the house."

At the mention of handgun Bolan looked up. He knew where Danson was going now and realized why Brognola had organized the meet with the undercover cop.

"So he's cooling his heels in lockup?"

"No. His girlfriend, Shayla, took the rap. Copped to it, said both were hers."

"Shayla? The girl he beat up?"

"Same one. A regular Romeo and Juliet, this pair. Only Shayla has a prior herself. A pandering charge that went to probation she got while the love of her life, Sideways, was upstate in prison."

"So she's in jail now?"

"Exactly, Sideways is drinking beer and screwing her little sister as we speak at the address that's in his file."

"And the handgun Newark copped on the raid?" Bolan asked. The question was rhetorical.

"An HS 2000 Croatian pistol," Danson confirmed.

Bolan nodded curtly. His finger found the button on the armrest of his car door and he began to power up the window.

"Looks like I need to pay our friend Sideways a little visit," he said.

"You tell Hal we're square now."

Bolan nodded before the window went up and then pushed the accelerator down on his car. Within a minute he had connected to the arterial and was gunning it across the overpass above his rendezvous site.

Jersey Shore

BOLAN LEFT THE CAR behind and merged with the night.

Sideways had made it easy for him. Or rather Shayla had. The house was surprisingly isolated. She'd taken her money from dancing and put it into a rundown, one-story Cape Cod overlooking the shore. It had been a fixer-upper with potential when she'd made the down payment on the house, but nothing had been improved and Sideways obviously wasn't the handyman type. Now the little white house merely looked shabby, with a weed-choked lawn and three Harley panheads parked under the lean-to that served as a garage.

Bolan moved up from the trees along the road, his movement masked by the droning of the cicadas and the sound of night surf battering the gray sand forty feet behind the old house.

Low lights were on in the house behind drawn shades, and the hard riffs of Metallica bled out through the closed windows and doors. The volume was surprisingly subdued given the biker stereotype.

Bolan, dressed in a blacksuit, crouched in the tall weeds at the edge of the yard. A massive pit bull was curled up on the front steps. It made soft snuffling noises as it slept. From where Bolan knelt the animal looked upward of eighty pounds of solid muscle. The soldier carefully unbuttoned the flap of the cargo pocket on his right pants leg and pulled out the plastic container Danson had given him and opened it.

Bolan took the two horse pills that had come with the meat and pried them apart, one after the other, and gently sprinkled their contents into the hamburger. Once he had spilled the tranquilizer powder into the meat he rolled it into a ball and held it loosely in his right hand.

He checked the wind coming in off the ocean, felt it push into his face. Satisfied, Bolan rose out of the weeds like a liquid shadow and lobbed the meatball in an arc over the thirty yards toward the front door of the one-story house.

The hamburger hit the walkway in front of the stairs with a muted little splat, and Bolan instantly folded himself back down into the weeds. The pit bull got to its feet in the blink of an eye, and Bolan could hear its deep-throated growl clearly. It sounded like the idling engines of one of the Harleys parked in the lean-to behind it.

The guard dog descended the wooden stair on stiffened legs, back hair bristling and teeth bared. Bolan remained motionless, draped in the night.

The dog suddenly stopped growling. Bolan saw the beast's snout suddenly shift as it caught the scent of the meat. Again the dog moved almost too fast to see, lunging forward and snapping up the ball of raw hamburger in a single chomp.

The dog worked the food around in its mouth, then swallowed it. With a last, suspicious glare into the night, it turned its nose and returned to the porch. It curled up again and went to sleep.

Bolan counted off the minutes on his wristwatch. He watched the dog's breathing first slow, then lengthen and deepen until he was sure the animal was securely drugged. Confident, Bolan rose and ghosted across the lawn toward the back of the house. The silenced Beretta was out from its shoulder holster and ready in his hands as he came up alongside the building.

He crept forward and reached a window, its blind not fully drawn. He stopped at the edge and slowly bent at the knees and lowered his body until he could peek under the shade and into the house through the dirty window.

Empty beer bottles were lined up on the end table four deep. Just beyond them he saw flickering images on a TV screen. A bed was positioned in front of the TV and Bolan recognized the woman on it from the file Danson had given him as Sheila, Shayla's younger sister and Sideways's current girlfriend. She was so skinny Bolan thought the pit bull might have outweighed her.

She opened her mouth and released the rubber tubing held between her teeth. Her eyes rolled back in her head as she pulled the empty hypodermic from her arm.

Grim-faced, Bolan turned away and continued toward the rear of the house. He cut through the lean-to, past the panheads and came around the corner where the smell of the sea was even stronger. He eased up to the screened-in back porch and took stock of the situation. Two men sat at a kitchen table drinking beer and shaking their heads in time to the music coming out of a boom box CD player on the counter next to a sink piled high with dirty dishes.

Bolan scrutinized the men through the open screen door. He recognized Sideways immediately. The man's gorilla arms hung from a cut-up flannel shirt and swirled with prison tats. A spiderweb had been tattooed on his elbow. The other guy was wearing an oil-stained sleeveless red T-shirt with an Aerosmith decal on the front. His long hair was held back in a ponytail. He was small only when compared to the massive Sideways.

A piece of glass, a double-edged razor blade and a generous mound of white powder were sitting on the table between the men. There was also a pistol. Bolan narrowed his eyes and took in the details of the handgun. It was a Croatian HS 2000.

The shorter man said something and Sideways snorted with laughter. He turned his head and called something out over his shoulder, obviously meant for the woman Bolan had seen dosing herself in the bedroom. When he got no answer, the frustrated biker stood abruptly, obviously pissed off, and stalked out through the kitchen doorway toward the front of the house. The second biker laughed to himself, then polished off his beer. He set down the empty and crossed the kitchen toward the refrigerator. As he bent to reach in and snatch up a full bottle of beer, he heard the screen door slam behind him. He straightened, a puzzled expression on his face as he turned.

Bolan stood before him.

"Who the fu—?" the man began.

Bolan slammed the butt of the stolen HS 2000 downward, and the end of the magazine cracked the biker across the nose. The big man crumpled at the knees and went down. A gash opened up across the bridge of his nose and spilled blood across his face.

Stunned, the biker rolled his eyes up and looked at the nightmare figure looming over him. Bolan slapped the muzzle of the pistol across the man's jaw, snapping his head to the side. With his face turned up like an offering, Bolan quickly snapped the Croatian handgun back then drove it forward, slamming the butt into the man's temple and putting his lights out.

Without uttering a word, the unconscious biker bounced off the fridge door and fell face-first onto the dirty kitchen floor. Bolan produced a pair of hinge-style handcuffs from his back pocket and quickly secured the man's hands behind his broad back. He could hear heavy footfalls approaching the kitchen from the front of the house, so he quickly moved beside the doorjamb.

Sideways stopped cold, incredulous shock stamped on his face, when he almost tripped over the unconscious and handcuffed body of his buddy lying on the floor.

Bolan stepped out and drove the muzzle of the HS 2000 Croatian pistol into the big man's solar plexus. Sideways grunted and folded like a cheap card table. As he went down, Bolan's knee came up and clipped him hard on the point of his chin.

Stunned by the second blow, Sideways flopped over on his back, hitting the dirty linoleum hard as he went down. In an instant Bolan was on him, shoving the gun into his face and pinning him to the floor with his other hand wrapped around the man's neck. Sideways's eyelids fluttered as he fought to regain his composure after the brutal ambush.

The Executioner's voice was like a cold wind through a high mountain pass as he spoke.

"I'm going to ask you some questions about where you got this pistol," Bolan said. "And you're going to tell me everything I want to know."

2

The squalid little Boston bar sat quiet and dark, caught between rundown residential neighborhoods on one side and the sprawling industrial wasteland surrounding a factory park on the other side.

The business was the kind of place that accepted food stamps and cashed welfare checks. On the first and fifteenth of every month it was a pretty lively place. It was early in the morning now, and the last of the homeless had been chased from the alleyway behind the one-story building. The tired old neon beer signs in the grimy front windows were turned off.

The only lights inside the tavern emanated from the crack beneath the door to the combination office and storage room in the back, just across from the entrance to the walk-in cooler. Muffled voices and sounds seeped out through the cheap wood along with the bar of pale yellow light.

Inside the room, against the far wall, crates of liquor devoid of tax stamps and cases of hijacked beer were stacked toward where Frankie Bonanno kept his desk, which was piled high with invoices, shipping recipes and defunct tax forms. A cheap accountant's calculator sat on the desktop next to an overflowing ashtray where a cigar smoldered.

Next to the ashtray was a lady's compact mirror with coke residue smeared across the glass and a sticky razor blade. Beside the mirror was a HS 2000 Compact Croatian handgun.

Just like Robert Scone, Frankie Bonanno was a big man. His forearms and shoulders were huge and hard from his time working the docks and cracking skulls. He was equally comfortable behind the controls of a forklift or swinging a sawed-off Louisville Slugger baseball bat. The knuckles on his hands had been broken so many times they were huge and misshapen.

His thin, greasy hair was swept back and plastered into place with the liberal use of gel in a vain attempt to cover an emerging bald spot the size of a tea saucer. His ruddy, acne-scarred complexion matched his alcoholic's broken-veined nose. His pig eyes were scrunched tightly in pleasure as the skinny blond woman's head bobbed up and down in his lap.

Suddenly the door to the office swung open in a swift arc and a living shadow rushed into the room. There was a whirl of dark fabric as a black overcoat came open and the masked specter's arms snaked out. The gloved hands were filled with deadly technology.

One hand swept downward and leveled a sound-suppressed Beretta 93-R on the huddled form of the cowering blonde. The left hand swung out from the intruder's coat and tracked straight onto the fat jowls and flabby chest of Frankie Bonanno.

Behind his mask Mack Bolan smiled.

There was a small mechanical click as Bolan's finger depressed the trigger on the stun gun and twin electrode darts fired out and hammered into Frankie Bonanno. There was a crackle as 2,000,000 volts sizzled into the big mobster. Immediately the sickly sweet stench of charred flesh filled the cramped little room.

Bonanno's shriek of pain morphed into a choking gurgle as he began to spasm and jerk in his seat, pants still down around his thick, hairy ankles. Blue bolts of electricity arced from the fillings in his teeth in an uncanny effect that produced a mouthful of fire.

Bolan hit the juice again and pushed another charge into the mobster.

The fat man looked up and saliva dribbled from his gaping mouth. Then there was a pause, two heartbeats long, as Bonanno slumped helpless in his chair.

Bolan turned his balaclava-covered face toward the cowering woman. "Get out," he ordered.

The woman looked up at the Executioner in stunned disbelief. Mob hitters were not known for compassion, and she clearly suspected some trick.

"I said get out!" Bolan snapped.

This time she did not hesitate. The woman scrambled to her feet and scurried to the door.

From the chair Frankie Bonanno lifted his head, still confused by the events unfolding around him.

"Who are—?" he began.

"Shut up," Bolan snapped. He pressed the cold muzzle of his Beretta against the oiled expanse of Bonanno's forehead. "If you so much as twitch I'll splatter your brains across the wall."

Frankie Bonanno froze. The mobster was deeply afraid. When the masked gunman had burst through the door, his first thought had been the Feds. But one man did not make up a SWAT team, federal or otherwise. A lone man meant a freelancer, and if that was true then Frankie wondered why he was still alive.

Bonanno watched as the figure in black pulled a pistol from behind his back. The handgun was identical to the weapon already sitting on the desk, a factory-new Croatian HS 2000 pistol. The man dropped it with a clatter that shattered the over-flowing ashtray and spilled cigarette butts across the desk and onto the floor.

The man dropped something smaller onto the desk between the two HS 2000 pistols. It was the size of a quarter and when Bonanno saw it lying there, an involuntary groan escaped him. His eyes showed sullen fear as they moved from the micro-processor chip on the desk back up to the intruder looming above him.

"Three months." Bolan said, voice harsh. "Three months ago a six-man team took down the supply dock of Las-Tech in Jersey. They got away with a shipment of chips just like that one. Chips that can run the supercomputers needed to control the centrifuges used to enrich uranium to weapons grade, say in Iran. Microprocessors sophisticated enough to turn scud missiles into guided munitions."

"I—I—" Bonanno's mouth worked uselessly as he tried to force his brain to come up with some lie that might save his life.

"Then suddenly a capo in Palermo has those same micro-chips on the open market and they go to an arms dealer in Bosnia, then multiple loads of Croatian pistols start flowing back through Palermo out of Sarajevo and into Jersey. And look, you happen to have one."

"Sarajevo is in Bosnia, not Croatia," Bonanno muttered.

Bolan stepped forward and cracked the butt of his Beretta across the mobster's face. His nose exploded and sprayed blood. His hand flew out and struck the open bottle of Jack Daniel's whiskey sitting on the desk and knocked it over. Amber fluid gurgled out of the bottle and began to spread across the desk.

"You think I need geography lessons from you?" Bolan asked, his voice flat. "Next time you get funny I put a bullet in your kneecap."

"I don't know anything—"

Frankie Bonanno's denial was cut short by the cough of the silenced Beretta in Bolan's hand. The slug slammed into the armrest of the mobster's chair, shattering wood with a sharp crack and driving splinters into the man's beefy arm.

Bonanno howled in agony.

Bolan stepped in close and leveled his pistol against Bonanno's broken, mashed nose.

"The name. Who facilitated the transfer through the Palermo capo and into Sarajevo?" Bolan's voice was soft.

Bonanno rolled his eyes toward the shiny, factory-new HS 2000 sitting on the desk just a few feet away, he knew it would do him no good. He inhaled breath through his pain and began to talk.

"Some guy," Bonanno said. "Got a Polack name or something. Taterczynski. Peter Taterczynski."

"How is he connected? Where does he work from?" Bolan fired his questions hard and fast, keeping the other man off balance.

"He's international, that's all I know. He used the Palermo capo because he wants a screen between himself and primarie's when it comes to operating in the States. The capo told my crew what to take, on spec."

"The microprocessors."

Bonanno nodded. "The microprocessors. Like I can move tech on my own? I deal in auto parts and cigarettes."

"So straight trade. Armed heist for tech you can't move in exchange for pistols you can."

"Yeah, basically."

"All set up by this player out of Sarajevo, Taterczynski?"

"Yeah, the Polack. But everything went through the Palermo capo's guy. A lieutenant, really scary dude name Paolini."

Bolan looked over at the desk where Bonanno's cell phone sat in the middle of the guns and the mess.

"You talk to this 'really scary' dude named Paolini on that phone?"

Bonanno nodded, his eyes hooded. They shifted past Bolan and suddenly he jerked upward toward the desk just as the hinges on the door behind them squeaked as it was thrown open.

Bolan caught a flash of motion as he shifted and twisted hard and felt the jerking tug of a knife blade catch in the tough polymer fibers of his Kevlar vest.

The soldier grunted in surprise as he reacted. It was the woman, back for some mad reason of her own and trying to save her tormentor in the vain hope of future favors. The knife in her hand was a big bladed kitchen utensil with a serrated edge, and she clearly aimed to kill Bolan with it.

The Executioner grabbed the overextended woman by the tangled hair at the back of her head and flung her hard to the ground. Frankie Bonanno was in motion, rising out of his seat and grasping for the butt of his loaded HS 2000 with a sweat-soaked hand. Bolan stepped forward and lashed out with one big, strong leg.

The heel of his low-cut boot ground against the mobster's wrist with an audible crunch on impact. The woman struggled to her feet, shrieking in rage, and threw herself at the black-clad intruder. Bolan drove his elbow backward into her soft belly and tossed her against the office wall. She slid down to the floor, her eyes rolling backward into her head. Bolan snapped his head back around as Bonanno reached for the HS 2000 pistol on his desk.

Bolan pivoted at the waist and fired three single shots into the fat man, pinning him to the seat, the Croatian pistol held uselessly in the man's uninjured hand. Frankie convulsed as his lungs deflated and the Croatian handgun discharged into his desk. Bonanno's eyes fluttered, and then a trickle of bright blood bubbled over his quivering lip and dribbled onto his chin.

Purposefully Bolan crossed to the desk and began to jerk open drawers. Casually he swept the mess on the desktop onto the floor. When the police came, they could make the link between the stolen tech and the smuggled pistols. Bolan would be several thousand miles ahead of any local investigation by the time they finished putting the pieces of the puzzle together.

He pocketed the dead man's cell phone, a virtual treasure trove of information, Bolan knew. Inside the desk he found a locked metal box. He swept up the container and smashed it against the edge of the desk, busting the cheap lock. Inside he found several grams of cocaine and two grand in worn twenties and fifties.

He stuffed the money into a pocket to add to his war chest. He turned and made for the office door, stepping over the sprawled form of the unconscious woman. He doubted if anyone outside would have heard the pistol shot, or that they would call the police if they had. Despite that it was sloppy fieldwork to tempt luck and Mack Bolan had not survived this long by being sloppy.

Bolan jerked the balaclava from his head as he stepped out the back door of the bar and into the alley. He moved forward, folding his black overcoat around him like a protective cloak of shadows. He navigated the filthy alley at a brisk pace and turned out onto a narrow street two blocks from the tavern.

He used his pocket remote to disengage the alarm on the black Prelude and it chirped once in response. He opened the door and slid into the vehicle.

Behind him the ocean mist swirled and crept along the littered ground as the Executioner sped away into the night.

3

Palermo, Italy

Bolan left the Palermo capo slumped dead across his desk and pocketed the flash drive that contained the information implicating Peter Taterczynski. As he exited the office, he could hear a pack of mafiosi approaching from the other direction. Bolan sprinted down the hallway, his Beretta 93-R clenched in his fist.

Behind him Bolan could hear the bodyguards closing in. A bullet screamed past his ear and smacked into the wall next to him. A heartbeat later he heard a chorus of pistol reports.

Bolan turned a corner in the hallway and bypassed the elevator banks in favor of the fire stairs. It hadn't been Paolini who had fired, he knew. Paolini wouldn't have missed.

The big American burst through the fire door and sprinted at breakneck speed down the stairs of the office building, stopping at each landing to vault the railing down to the level of stairs. He had purposefully chosen the east wing of the building as his escape route, knowing it would be deserted and minimizing the chance that innocents would be caught in any cross fire.

Bolan was three floors down by the time his pursuers hit the stairwell. One of the thugs leaned over the railing and loosed a 3-round burst from his HS 2000 automatic pistol at Bolan's retreating form.

Paolini barked an angry warning to his subordinate and reached out to pull him back from the railing. The man came away easily, his head jerking sharply from an unseen impact. The back of his skull erupted, spraying the other six gunmen with blood and brain and bits of bone.

"Fool!" Paolini snarled.

Furious, the Mob lieutenant jumped past the corpse of his soldier, the other thugs following his lead. Their speed was now marked with a certain caution that bordered on outright hesitancy.

THREE FLOORS BENEATH THEM Bolan ran on. The time would come to kill Paolini, but for now he had to escape to advance his operation. He had his eyes set on something bigger than a recently deceased Palermo capo with international influence; Bolan would pursue the Sarajevo connection and the possibility of an American traitor.

He barreled down the stairs to the fifth floor, where he abandoned the stairwell in favor of the door leading into the warren of halls that was the east wing.

The building itself had served the Palermo capo with a veneer of legitimacy, housing the offices of his credit union, construction firm, as well as his shipping and air-freight operations. When Bolan had agreed to meet the kingpin there, he knew full well he was walking into a trap.

Halfway down the hall Bolan came to a four-way intersection. He paused, weighing his options—flight or ambush?

Bolan smiled; Paolini was vain. He thought he knew all the tricks, but Paolini was just a pup for all of his violent accomplishments. It was the Executioner who was the master of hounds.

PAOLINI WASN'T the first gunner through the door.

Two of his men, Yeats and Delgaro, entered first. Yeats came in high and on the right, swinging forward with his HS 2000 Croatian pistol and laying down a hailstorm of covering fire. The weapon jumped and kicked in his hand, scattering hot shell casings onto the floor.

Delgaro was the low man, his own pistol poised to provide supporting fire. A thunderous silence echoed along the hallway as their prey neglected to return fire.

"He's gone rabbit!" Delgaro said.

He pointed down the corridor toward the intersection of hallways.

Yeats's face split into a smile, his teeth blunt and very white against the darker complexion of his skin. He put a finger to his lips to silence his partner and pointed. Paolini came through the doorway and peered over Yeats's shoulder. He looked down the hall to where the subordinate was indicating.

"You better be right," he whispered, his lips close to the man's ear. "Now slide on up to that corner and take a look, little sister."

Yeats bristled at Paolini's mocking tone. The capo's lieutenant was always testing the crew, establishing his dominance in little ways, pushing them to see if they would snap or if he could provoke emotion. It didn't matter to him that each man had made his bones with the organization a dozen times over before being promoted to the capo's bodyguard. Paolini was never satisfied, and with his minutes-old promotion to the top slot, Yeats knew it wasn't likely to get any better.

Yeats sighed and began to move forward, clearing the corner with Delgaro, using rudimentary but practical tactics. Unlike Paolini, none of the other hitters had formal military training, only street experience. Still, the men had picked up a lot as targets of Italian anti-Mafia government raiders.

Yeats's head exploded like an overripe melon.

Dellavechia and Montenegro died in the next second. Delgaro screamed in fear and flung himself down to his belly on the blood-slick linoleum floor. Behind him Paolini grabbed up Yeats's falling corpse and swung it around to use as a shield.

A hitter named Vincenetti had time to turn, dropping low in a combat crouch and swinging around on one knee, his HS 2000 pistol outfitted with a laser sight that burned down the hall, tracking for a target.

Vincenetti saw the black-clad form of the crazy bastard who'd dropped the Palermo capo in his own building. The Italian gunman lined up the sights of his handgun and his finger flexed around the plastic-alloy curve of his Croatian pistol. He *had* the bastard.

Vincenetti was too slow, and Paolini had another corpse at his feet. An untidy third eye blossomed in Vincenetti's forehead.

Delgaro was sweating, pressed flat against the floor and panting in fear. Their adversary had gunned down four experienced killers in the blink of an eye.

For the first time since the hunt had begun, Delgaro thought about just running. He no longer cared if the kill was personal. Screw avenging the capo, screw pride and screw honor. He just wanted to live, goddammit.

"Get up!" Paolini snarled at the prostrate man.

Delgaro looked up, and Paolini pushed the bullet-riddled corpse of Yeats away from him. It fell to the linoleum floor with a wet slap like a bag of loose meat. Delgaro realized that as terrified as he was of the apparition that had brought hell to Palermo, he was still frightened of his lieutenant.

He scrambled to his feet, following Paolini down the hall to the elevators, trusting the ex-Foreign legionnaire's instincts.

Delgaro had never seen anything like the ambush before in his life, not ever and not even close. Even the Chechens didn't kill like that and they were fucking crazy, he knew.

DELGARO TURNED toward Paolini where he had paused at the elevators.

"Those are service elevators. They'll take him all the way down into the underground parking lot or even the storage basement. He may have gone there," Paolini explained. He looked around, his HS 2000 pistol up and ready. "Or he could still be on this floor. We should split up."

"Maybe it would be better if—" Delgado began.

Paolini looked at the other man, cutting him off. "You take the elevator—I'll check out this level."

Delgaro swallowed, trying to get hold of himself. He had survived some hairy plays, including pulling weapons for drugs deals with the crazy Chechens. He could be cool. It just wasn't every day he saw five top gunners go down. It wasn't every day he faced an old-fashioned cowboy.

"Right," he forced himself to say and nodded.

Delgaro ejected his old magazine and slapped a fresh one home. He turned toward the elevator, well aware the mystery killer in black could be in there, waiting.

He resisted the urge to tell Paolini to cover him; it was obvious the man would, he hoped. Delgaro was a pro at urban close-quarters battle. His knowledge had been earned right out on the Palermo streets surrounding this very building.

Delgaro slid up next to the elevator doors and pressed his back tightly against the wall. He looked across the lobby and saw Paolini positioned directly opposite the elevator doors, down on one knee with his HS 2000 held steady in both hands.

Keeping his own pistol up, Delgaro used the thumb of his left hand to punch the control button on the wall, opening the elevator doors. They slid open with a hydraulic hiss and he dived onto his shoulder, rolling across his back to land flat on his stomach in front of the opening. His HS 2000 was tensed in his hand, ready to explode in violent action.

Behind him Paolini tensed so suddenly he almost seemed to flinch, coming very close to accidentally triggering his weapon.

The elevator car was empty.

Paolini relaxed as Delgaro straightened.

"All right," the brand-new capo growled. "Check out the basement below us. I'll call my guy on the force and get some cops who are part of our thing to respond. I'll look out up here—we've got to keep him in the building. Now go."

"You get that backup." Delgaro nodded.

The mafioso stepped into the elevator. His last image before the doors closed was of Paolini's angular face, tightly smiling and impossible to read. Paolini's a cobra, Delgaro realized. Just a poisonous reptile.

Delgaro didn't see the hatch on the elevator ceiling slide open, nor did he hear the slight popping of joints as the Executioner straightened his arm out, his deadly Beretta in a steady hand.

Delgaro moved to one side and pressed himself flat against the side of the elevator, his pistol up and ready in hands slick with sweat. He wasn't about to be caught like a rabbit out of its hole when those doors slid open.

The elevator bell rang as the car settled. There was the familiar slight hiss of air as the doors unsealed and slid open. The discreet cough of the Beretta was lost in those sounds.

The mobster's head smacked up against the elevator wall. A ragged hole appeared in his temple, and the other side of his head cracked open and sprayed his brains out. The mafioso gunner slid down to crumple on the floor, a trail of crimson smeared on the wall behind him. The pistol fell out of his slack fingers and bounced off the floor.

Mack Bolan had just done what the Chechens had never been able to do.

4

If pressed, Stephen Caine couldn't pinpoint when things had begun to fall apart. Not just the gradual erosion of his personal life, but the future of the entire country grew bleaker by the day as his anger and bitterness consumed him.

It was a lot like Chinese water torture, Caine decided. Just this slow *drip, drip, drip* that built up over time until each drop felt like a ball-peen hammer and sounded like thunder. Every day something else happened, another loss, a fresh insult, and his frustration had become intolerable.

Things started happening and he couldn't really remember doing them, not fully anyway. He didn't black out, but he operated on autopilot for so much of the day that decisions he made on the edge of sleep would be fully formed and operational plans by the time the morning came around. On his own, he felt helpless to act. A majority of the people who actually made the effort to vote had chosen wrong, had bought into the bullshit and the spin machine and now everything was spiraling out of control.

Caine set the empty shot glass of bourbon on the bar and eased down a few swallows of his Bud Light to cool the burning in the pit of his stomach. He knew he was a cliché. Strangely, that realization really didn't make him feel any better.

The bar was working class, which he definitely wasn't, but slumming made him feel better. His father would have been right at home here, smoking unfiltered cigarettes and downing bourbon like water while watching the flickering images of sports on the TV above the bar. Caine had learned everything he believed about politics by listening to what his father said and then doing the opposite.

A talking head on the TV was explaining why collateral damage wasn't the same as those killed by deliberate acts of terrorism. The bartender moved over and took Caine's empty shot glass. She was forty and skinny and tired. She had a plain face and a smoker's squint. Caine had forgotten her name.

"You want another shot?" she asked.

"Let me ask you something," Caine said.

She looked down the bar at the handful of other customers to see if they were happy. Once she decided they were fine she turned back toward Caine. Her eyes were green.

"What's that?"

"You know what the electoral college is for?"

"You think you're funny? You think I'm stupid 'cause I tend bar so you can ask me these questions then laugh at me?"

Caine blinked in surprise. Whatever he'd been expecting that wasn't it.

"No," he answered her. "I don't think that. I was using the question as a lead-in, more of a rhetorical thing, so I could pontificate. You know, like drunks are supposed to do."

The bartender looked at Caine, evaluating him. She picked up the empty shot glass and placed it in the steel-lined sink behind the bar.

"Fine," she said. "The electoral college are the ones who actually cast the votes for the President, right? They look at the popular vote for their state, then cast the votes of their electoral college for the person who won the popular vote."

"But they don't have to," Caine said. He was starting to feel the bourbon now.

This caught the woman by surprise, and she gave him a look like he was trying to be sly.

"No, it's true." Caine laughed. "They are free to cast the electoral votes for whomever they wish. They don't, by law, have to cast them for whoever wins the popular vote."

"That true?" she asked.

Caine smiled up at her. "Pour me another good one, if you please." He slid a twenty across the bar, and the bartender smoothly went through her motions. "Supposedly it's because of demagogues," he continued.

He slid the hard liquor down his throat with a smooth, practiced motion. He reflected that there was a handgun in his car. He didn't believe in guns, not anymore, but it was there, in the trunk. There was no way Charisa would ever have let it into the house, but Charisa wasn't there anymore. He'd lost his wife and gained a gun.

How great was that?

Of course he didn't have the house anymore, either. The settlement had been very clear; they split the house right down the middle. Didn't much matter that the slimeball lawyer she'd left him for had a sprawling ranch-style twice the size of their old fixer-upper.

"Why?" the bartender repeated.

"What?" Caine blinked up at her.

"Why demagogues?" She sounded exasperated. "You were talking about the electoral college, remember?"

Caine gave her a dour smile and shrugged. The bartender snorted and dismissed him, moving down the bar. Someone came into the bar from the outside, and Caine realized it had started to rain.

He left a good tip by way of apology and headed out the door. Outside the rain turned everything gray. He couldn't stop thinking about Charisa, about everything he'd lost.

He would never get her back, he knew. Would never get back his Army buddies who'd fallen in Mogadishu, either. Or his brother, Justin, who'd joined the Marines and never came back from Iraq.

But if Stephen Caine couldn't get justice, he'd get revenge. Someone would pay.

5

Vincent Paolini had held everything he'd ever wanted in his hands before he lost it all. He'd worked his way out of his childhood of rural poverty and to the university at Naples on a soccer scholarship. His soccer playing had been good enough to make old men cry and present him with an unending parade of female admirers.

But if blood could tell, then it told in Vincent Paolini's case.

He was the son of a fifth-generation made man, and he'd learned in the cradle that anyone who pissed off a Paolini had to pay. He'd beaten an American sailor to death in the waterfront bar of Ravenna with a pool cue. Just like that his future as a European professional soccer player had disappeared.

He'd fled, and his friends had covered for him enough to obstruct the investigation. He joined the Spanish foreign legion, the lesser known refuge of rogues and desperate men than the French version, but just as brutal and just as elite.

He'd done three years in the Spanish legion while memories in Italy faded. He'd hunted the Taliban in Afghanistan, served as peacekeeper in Bosnia and in Liberia. He'd been trained as a light infantry commando and had been in dozens of firefights.

During that time his father, now an old man retired to his vineyards and dog breeding, appealed to the Palermo capo. In return for certain services, the capo had promised to use his influence to bury the investigation of the American sailor's death.

Paolini had killed three people, two men, one a World War II veteran, and a woman to clear his debt. By that time he'd found he had a flair for the Family business and he'd risen to the position of the capo's right-hand man.

Now, thanks to the mystery hitter, Vincent Paolini *was* the Palermo capo. Right now the Palermo capo felt something he thought he'd put behind him in the mountains of Afghanistan: fear.

He was afraid he'd gotten cocky, telling himself that despite the smooth ambush the mystery killer had pulled off, Paolini was still the better killer.

Had he been wrong?

He'd just seen five hardened killers gunned down in less than ten minutes. He hadn't seen carnage on that scale since he'd witnessed the ethnic cleansing in Africa as a legionnaire. The guy was good, Paolini admitted. But, dammit, he was better—he had to believe that.

He had to.

BOLAN'S MUSCLES STRAINED and jumped beneath his skin as he climbed hand-over-hand up the elevator shaft, clinging to the thick cables like a spider to its web. He'd sent the elevator up a few floors, pressing multiple buttons so that the passenger car would stop at every floor in between. Once the elevator was in motion, Bolan had pried open the shaft doors and begun his journey upward. He hoped the ruse would give him enough time to hunt down and catch an angle on Paolini.

He knew that common sense told him to take his information and run. The Palermo capo's operation had been thrown into disarray, and Bolan had what he needed to move up the food chain toward his ultimate prize. The payoff was bigger if Stony Man exploited the information he'd obtained than if he killed a single Italian Mob lieutenant.

But he was going to do it anyway.

PAOLINI STOOD IN THE SHADOWS and watched the elevator going up, plotting its progress by the lighted numerals above the doors. The lift had stopped on his floor, and the doors slid open to reveal nothing more than Delgaro's bloody corpse. The doors slid shut again and the elevator rose. When it finally halted, Paolini had recalled it and, stepping inside, had quickly pushed the button to send the elevator all the way back down before stepping out.

All the way down to the basement.

He snickered. If the mystery gunman was doing what Paolini suspected, then he'd be squashed flatter than a bug under his heel. That is a sign of old age, Paolini thought, predictability. In their business, the business of professional killers, that was a fatal flaw. In the future Paolini intended to make sure he didn't make the same mistakes.

BOLAN LOOKED UP as he heard the elevator kick into life, and he knew he had mistimed his trick. It was a potentially fatal mistake, but he'd known the risk when he played his gambit and he was prepared to live or die by his instincts.

He scrambled up the service ladder set into the shaft. Above him the bottom of the elevator smoothly powered down toward him. He was in a race, climbing against the clock, and now time had run out. He'd tried to play Paolini for a fool and had been off by a good thirty seconds.

That could prove to be a lifetime.

Realizing he would have to climb faster if he wanted to make it, Bolan stopped to replace his Beretta in his shoulder holster. His right hand slid the muzzle of the weapon into the sling as his left wrapped around the rung just above his head.

The metal rung was covered in some cold, slimy fluid. Perhaps it was maintenance oil or some other service fluid; in the dim light Bolan couldn't tell. His hand slid off the slick metal, surprising him, and he overbalanced. His hands flung outward and one foot slipped off the rung below him. As he scratched for purchase his pistol fell away.

Darkness enveloped him as he fell, bouncing off the walls of the elevator shaft. His hands reached out to grasp the rungs of the service ladder. His sudden stop pushed him roughly up against the sheer metal wall again, forcing air from his lungs. His head slammed forward and his lip was split against the steel ladder.

The agony was a sharp, sudden shock and his tenuous grip weakened and then slipped. He fell backward down the shaft for a second time. His leg was jerked cruelly in its socket and he came to a brutally abrupt halt, his ankle twisted in one of the rungs.

Hot spears of pain lanced through his leg and muscles and tendons shrieked in protest at the tension.

Above him the elevator raced down.

Bolan reached up with one strong hand to pull himself back up. His face was sticky with blood from his nose, and his lips were bloody and swollen as he fought to regain control of his breath.

Bolan fought himself up into a vertical position. Standing on the ladder, favoring one leg, he stretched out a blood-smeared hand and pried his fingers into the rubber buffer curtain set between the floor-level doors.

The muscles along his back and shoulders bunched under the strain. With a final desperate exertion, the top half of the fingernail on his middle finger was ripped away, but the doors came open under his grip.

He looked up. The bottom of the elevator was in plain sight, rushing down toward his upturned face. Bolan tensed then sprang off the ladder rung, reaching out for the opening. He scrambled through the opening just as the elevator filled the space directly above him.

Adrenaline shot through his body, and Bolan found the desperate strength he needed to live. He pulled himself through the opening just as the elevator dropped past him. He had made it.

PAOLINI STRUCK the Executioner like a runaway locomotive, driving him back into the open shaft. Their momentum was greater than the elevator's and they hit the roof of the carrier hard. They fell like squabbling cats, punching and striking at each other as they dropped.

In the split second before they smashed into the elevator roof, Bolan managed to twist his enemy beneath him so that he landed on top of the capo. Paolini kicked his adversary away from him, knocking him back across the elevator roof to the other side of the lift. Bolan rebounded off the wall of the shaft and bounced forward to his knees before coiling and leaping to his feet.

Both men sprang forward and, locked together, they struggled as the elevator descended to the basement.

When Bolan had been in the Army, he'd undergone training in defense against attack dogs. The premise had been as simple as it was brutally effective. You gave the animal an arm, knowing it would be bit, then the free arm came down like a bar and wrapped around the back of the dog's head where the skull met spine. The man then fell forward and the beast's neck snapped like a stick of rotten wood.

Bolan's arms broke the clinch and one forearm pressed hard against the Italian's face. His other arm slid into place behind the man's neck, right where the skull met the spine. He began to push.

Paolini could feel his neck begin to break. Terror lent him a superhuman strength but to no avail. His huge fists hammered into Bolan's midriff, his knee attempted to maul Bolan's crotch, but the Executioner ignored the blows, the damage, the pain.

The elevator settled into position on the ground with a subtle lurch, just enough to cause Bolan's injured leg to buckle. He tripped back and fell through the open maintenance hatch, dropping straight down through to the elevator compartment below.

His purchase suddenly gone, Paolini tumbled forward, as well. His momentum carried him down through the elevator hatch to land on top of Bolan. A backward elbow caught the Italian in the face, stunning him for a second as Bolan lunged for the pistol lying on the floor next to Delgaro's limp hand.

Bolan lifted the pistol just as the elevator doors slid open and Paolini's heel cracked hard against his wrist, sending the handgun spinning off out of the compartment. Bolan twisted back toward the Mob enforcer and saw him clawing his own Croatian HS 2000 out of a shoulder sling. Bolan brought a hammer-hard fist up from the hip and smashed it into Paolini's temple, staggering the man as he tried to rise to his knees.

Bolan's other hand lanced out and tried to take the pistol from Paolini. The two men struggled for control of the weapon. Bolan drew back his left hand to strike the other man again.

Paolini squeezed the trigger, and 9 mm rounds riddled the roof and walls of the elevator as he continued jerking the trigger. The pistol bucked and kicked in their hands as Bolan tried to wrestle it free, slugs stitching a crooked line across the wall toward the control panel.

Three soft-nosed slugs smacked into the delicate electronics and chewed their way through the thin outer casing. The elevator doors finished sliding open as sparks flew in rooster tails. The lights went out the instant Paolini pulled the trigger on the final bullet in the handgun.

Once again darkness enveloped Bolan.

Paolini swung wildly in the darkness, his knuckles clipping Bolan on the chin. The American's head snapped back and he rolled with the force of the blow, letting it carry him back away from the mafioso.

As he finished his backward somersault, he felt the cool hardness of a concrete floor. He had cleared the elevator, but the basement was as dark as a tomb.

Bolan rose and reached out a hand to either side of him in the pitch blackness. He walked quickly forward, lifting his feet high and putting them down flat to avoid tripping in the dark. Despite his precaution, he nearly tripped over some obstacle and he used the noise to dodge hard to the left, coming up against a wall.

He pressed his back against the structure, his ears straining to catch any sound. Silence was the key. When you fought with one sense gone the surest way to victory was to deprive your opponent of his other senses.

He stood motionless, fighting to control his breathing, painfully aware of how loud his ragged, gasping breath had to be. After what felt like an eternity he regained control of his body.

Holding his breath, Bolan strained to listen.

Soon the sound of his own blood rushing in his ears deafened him to the point that he was defeating his original purpose. Slowly he exhaled, struggling to keep the escaping breath silent.

Then he heard it. He heard Paolini breathe. He couldn't be sure, but it had seemed, in that instant, that Paolini was no more than a few yards from him.

Bolan began to move. He kept his back flat against the wall, his hands reaching out far to the sides to feel for obstacles. He moved slowly, crossing one leg over the other. He swallowed tightly, concentrating on pinpointing Paolini's exact location.

Five steps and then he halted. He could hear no sound. Tension gripped him, but only for a moment. Bolan had spent too many years on the hellgrounds to be killed by indecision.

He swallowed tightly and then stepped away from the safety of the wall. He couldn't hear Paolini moving, and he froze. After a short while he heard the strained outlet of escaping breath and realized Paolini had been listening for him.

In the deep darkness of the basement Bolan had his enemy pinpointed. He stepped forward and reached a sprint in three quick strides. Bolan leaped into the air, thrusting out both feet before him.

His injured leg struck Paolini in the gut, driving the younger man's arm into his own stomach and forcing the air from him. Bolan's other leg struck the cinder-block wall Paolini had been standing against and buckled under the force of impact.

Bolan bounced away, striking the floor on his rebound. Paolini fell beside him and the Executioner rose, smashing his fist down. He nearly cried out in pain as his knuckles struck the concrete floor and his arm went instantly numb.

He heard a sharp crack and instinctively threw up his good arm to ward off the invisible blow. His forearm jerked under the force of some club, probably a snapped-off broom handle.

Intuiting Paolini's position by the angle of the blow, Bolan whipped his legs around and he felt the Italian topple. He heard Paolini's club clatter away as he slammed to the floor, and Bolan snatched up the weapon for himself.

Bolan didn't hesitate. He rose to one knee and brought the stolen stick crashing down. The stick splintered along its length from the force of the blow on Paolini's body.

Paolini responded like a fighter, lashing out quickly. The ball of his foot slapped into Bolan's face, driving him backward with the blunt force of a sledgehammer.

Bolan felt fresh blood hot in his mouth as his bottom lip was cut by his own teeth. Again he used the energy to roll with the blow and disengage, flipping over backward and gaining his feet. He tripped and fell back, landing hard on his butt with a jar that seemed to loosen his teeth in his head. He blinked in surprise. He was sitting up higher than the floor. He reached behind and realized he was on a flight of stairs.

Bolan turned and scrambled up the steps, racing so fast that his head butted against the door. He yanked at the knob.

It was locked.

Bolan felt around the walls, found what he was looking for and the lights came on as he flicked the switch. He blinked in the sudden illumination and looked behind him. Paolini was at the bottom of the staircase, a jagged-ended broom handle in his fists. The left side of his face was a long purple bruise where Bolan had struck him with his own club.

As Paolini began to slowly climb the steps, his eyes never left Bolan's for an instant. "You're mine now, hardass," he growled. "I'm gonna jam this stick in your heart."

Paolini raced up the last few steps and jabbed the splintered end of the stick forward in an attempt to stab Bolan. The Executioner dodged to the side and kicked Paolini in the face. Weakened, the man tumbled down the stairs rolling end over end.

The mobster hit the bottom step at a wrong angle, and

Bolan heard the snap of the Italian's neck as it broke. The Mob lieutenant plopped into an unceremonious pile of tangled limbs at the bottom of the stairs.

Bolan quickly descended and confirmed the kill.

Then he turned to collect his weapons and search for an exit route.

6

The day that Stephen Caine quit his job he didn't tell anyone he was going. He wouldn't need the job; it would only slow him.

He walked out of his office and to the elevator. He wanted a drink. Inside the elevator he suddenly realized he couldn't remember what his office looked like. Couldn't remember the faces of the people there, or their names.

He wanted a drink, but he didn't want to return to the blue collar bar. He didn't belong there. His father would have belonged there and so, by definition he didn't belong there. He was going to go some place upscale but mellow, maybe with a piano player.

In the Explorer, on the way to the lounge, Caine began to cry. The tears streamed down his face in salty rivers. Six casualties a day. All of them dying just like his buddy Angel Ramos had in Mogadishu: hard and bloody.

In the car Caine remembered the medicine the Army doctors had given the men of the unit upon rotating home, just until the nightmares and flashbacks had stopped, or subsided anyway. He figured there *had* to be several dozen pills out there that could help trip the switch to stop the images, stop the tears. He didn't think the doctors would hesitate to give him some pills if he told them about Mogadishu.

The piano bar was quiet and open but comfortably dark, and Caine didn't look out of place in his suit with loosened tie. He drank straight through into evening and met the hooker once the sun had gone down.

Her name was Stephanie, and he was pretty sure from the start that she was a call girl. She was beautiful and didn't look anything like Charisa and, unlike Charisa, she didn't seem to have a problem getting blasted with him. He got his first Xanax from her, a little pill she fished out of the bottom of her Versace handbag. He watched the way the ends of her long brown hair rubbed across the smooth curves of her spilling cleavage while she dug for the pill. She smelled really good, and after she gave him the antianxiety medicine he decided she could really be into him. He washed the pill down with a swallow of imported beer.

"Because of demagogues," he finished.

"Demagogues?" she asked.

"Yes, demagogues. A political leader who gains power by appealing to people's emotions, instincts and prejudices in a way that is considered manipulative and dangerous…to paraphrase."

"So you're saying the President is a demagogue."

"Yes. The problem is that the electoral college failed. The system is flawed. It is flawed because we only have a two-party system. The parties that control the electoral college are partisan. So maybe they would vote to check a demagogue who was an independent, but never to check one from within their own party. Without agreement, which is impossible in partisan atmospheres, the electoral college could never keep out a demagogue if they emerged from one of the two ruling political parties. The system fails."

"That's democracy." Stephanie shrugged. She seemed to be tuning him out, bored. But Caine was talking mainly to hear his own voice anyway. What he was planning was a big deal, and it scared the hell out of him. The Xanax seemed to help.

Stephanie's eyes were like glass marbles and her words came out softly slurred.

"But if democracy had ever been intended to be a simple mob rule then the founding fathers never would have inserted the electoral college into the process to begin with," he continued. "It is a part of the system. The system failed." And six a day are dying because of it, Caine thought to himself.

"What are you going to do?"

"Well, Thomas Jefferson had a few ideas...." Caine trailed off and took a drink.

Her hand came to rest on his thigh and the scent of a sensuous perfume drifted over him. He felt himself respond and knew what he wanted, even though he understood what Stephanie was.

"I meant tonight," she purred. The purr was as slurred as her words.

Caine looked over at Stephanie and smiled. He felt warm and detached, and he knew now that if he needed to do something then it would be much later and he would be detached enough to do it then, too.

Thomas Jefferson had known what to do about demagogues, but Caine would be doing it in his own way. The plan started to coalesce in his mind as he stared into Stephanie's eyes. He was not yet sure what it involved, but he was certain it would get to the truth, to the pattern that ran beneath the surface.

"You ready to get out of here?" she asked.

"Yes," he answered, "I'm ready."

The sudden resolve in his voice suggested he was talking more to himself than to Stephanie.

7

Mack Bolan was back in Sarajevo, the capital of Bosnia and Herzegovina, autonomous states of the former Yugoslavia Republic. While Bosnia maintained diplomatic ties with the United States, it held no extradition treaty and criminals with the financial resources and political connections had found haven from American justice within its borders.

One such man was Peter Taterczynski, former State Department intelligence analyst and Department of Defense contractor. Two years earlier he had ended two decades of public service after his wife walked out on him, taking the children and sixty percent of his income in alimony and court-mandated child support. His hard drinking and prolific affairs had stalled his career at the middle-management level and ruined his domestic life. He had brought his own ruin upon himself.

In response he had used a hidden camera to procure copies of sensitive documents from the National Archives, including counterintelligence files listing active U.S. agents in a host of former Soviet republics and Middle Eastern countries. He had fled with this information first to Munich and then on to Sarajevo.

Between the sales of the sensitive information and his ability to produce American end-user certificates for international arms sales he had made a tidy sum. He had used some of his newfound money to secure a patron in the Bosnian foreign ministry. This protection, married to the lack of an extradition treaty, had put him beyond the reach of traditional law enforcement and diplomatic resources.

In Syria alone thirteen agents were exposed and murdered as a result of his treason. Although Peter Taterczynski remained beyond the reach of the law, beyond the reach of justice, he was not beyond the reach of the Executioner.

After arriving at the international airport, Bolan headed to the concierge's desk to pick up a key left under an alias that matched his passport. The pretty woman in a Sarajevo Airlines uniform smiled at him and checked his ID. Her eyes flitted across the cut of his nondescript but expensive suit.

"Are you in Sarajevo for business or pleasure?" she asked.

"Business, I'm afraid," Bolan replied.

"Well, I hope your trip is successful," she answered, handing him the envelope containing the little key.

"Thank you."

The key belonged to a small storage locker in the luggage area. Inside was a parking slip and ignition key to Bolan's mission vehicle, a black Lexus. The Lexus had been upgraded with a diplomatic protection kit that included a V8 engine, tinted and bullet-resistant windows, body armor, self-sealing tires, a satcom uplink phone with encryption device and GPS unit.

Bolan programmed in the coordinates to the target site that he had memorized after removing a Beretta 93-R from the glove box and attaching the sound suppressor. He set the deadly pistol on the passenger's seat beside him and pulled out onto the road.

Fifteen minutes later he was ready and in position.

THE TAUPE MERCEDES ENTERED the underground garage, rolling forward down the ramp on fat, high-performance tires with its high beams on. Bolan slid the silenced Beretta 93-R behind his back. The Mercedes rolled to a stop and the driver killed the lights. The two luxury vehicles sat facing each other with twenty yards of parking lot between them. After a moment the door to the Mercedes popped open and a tall thin man in an expensive suit climbed out.

Bolan opened the door to his car and did the same. He walked out from behind the open door to his vehicle and regarded the Iranian intelligence agent. The man was bald with a neatly groomed beard and mustache showing patches of gray. In his hands was a burgundy leather attaché case.

"You are not Taterczynski!" the Iranian swore.

He dropped the attaché case to the concrete, where it made a loud, flat slapping sound. The Iranian's hand flew inside his suit jacket and under his arm. Bolan reached around behind him and grabbed the smooth butt of his machine pistol.

Bolan was dropping down to one knee as he pulled his weapon free and he saw the Iranian produce a Glock 19. The Executioner fired and the Beretta jumped in his fist delivering a 3-round burst. Spent shell casings tumbled out and bounced off the concrete.

The Iranian stumbled backward and blossoms of scarlet appeared on his white-linen shirt over his chest. His leg caught the corner of the still-running Mercedes and he went down, arms windmilling.

The Glock tumbled from his hands, bounced off the bumper of the car and struck the ground next to the attaché case. Blood spilled across both items in fat, dime-sized drops. The man hit the floor with a heavy, wet sound and his head bounced with a hollow smack. The dying man's left foot spasmed once, then he relaxed as his final breath escaped his body.

Bolan rose slowly from his knee, pistol held ready in his hands. He walked over toward the attaché case lying at the man's feet and picked it up, heedless of the blood splatters. It represented the quintessential forty pieces of silver any Judas demanded for his services.

Bolan walked back to his car and threw the money-filled case onto the passenger's seat. He climbed in behind the wheel, slammed the door and keyed the ignition. He drove past the dead man and out into the night without a second glance.

The soldier picked up the sat phone from the console and hit the speed dial. The person on the other end of the line answered on the first ring.

"Striker here," Bolan said. "The interdiction was a success. The subject was completely surprised I wasn't the principal. I'm in route to alpha location now. Tell Bear he did good work with the set up."

Bolan listened for a moment. "I will," he answered. "Call with an update later. Striker out."

Bolan used his thumb to kill the connection and he tossed the phone onto the seat beside him next to the attaché case.

THE CENTRAL INTELLIGENCE Agency had done Bolan's grunt work for him. Stringers, agents and confidential informants saturated the former Yugoslavia Republic. The Kosovo Police Service had been created in 1999 in the aftermath of the NATO bombing campaign and subsequent withdrawal of the Yugoslav and Serbian forces from Kosovo. The former leader of Serbia had previously purged most Albanians from the police in Kosovo, and because of this, when Serbian forces withdrew, there were no longer any police officers to maintain public order in Kosovo. The establishment of the United Nations Interim Administration Mission in Kosovo—UNMIK— included a large international policing component, named the UNMIK Police. Their two primary tasks were to establish a new police force and in the meantime to maintain civil law and order.

The United Nations police force was filled with former U.S. law-enforcement agents from the state, local and federal levels serving not only as patrolmen but also as trainers. The UN police force provided equipment, weapons, instruction, communications gear and even uniforms to the host nation. Several of the deployed trainers and officers had served as stalking horses for U.S. intelligence concerns. As a result Stony Man Farm had access to the CIA's list of pay-for-play officers.

In short, Bolan knew exactly whom to bribe.

THE NIGHT HAD GROWN darker as Bolan surveyed the ship secured to the pier. The vessel was small as freighters went at two thousand five hundred tons and running two hundred feet prow to stern by thirty feet across the main deck. Carefully, Bolan chose his route of infiltration.

He crossed the yard and hit the dock, moving quickly to crouch near a huge pilling in the shadow of the ship. The smell of the quay was strong, a mix of salt and fish and mildew, along with the odor of floating garbage and rotting wood.

Off to his left from the aft of the ship he saw a single wharf rat scramble across a thick mooring rope of woven hemp. From the side of the ship an automatic bilge pump began spilling yellowish water in a stream out of a small port.

Unconsciously Bolan reached up and touched the pistol butt of his Beretta 93-R where it rode in a holster under his arm. His eyes scanned the ship, narrowed to slits. Taterczynski had made Bolan's job easier by choosing the sort of company he now kept. The former analyst had handpicked a small cadre of former Bosnian commandos linked to units accused of the worst crimes: ethnic cleansing, torture, rape camps, the sniping of civilians and relief workers.

Bolan would show them no mercy.

His gaze roamed over the deck and across the superstructure. The big windows fronting the bridge were dark, and he could detect no activity. Bolan remained motionless, as patient as a hunter in ambush. There would be a guard. A man like Taterczynski always had a guard.

Wearing a peacoat and watch cap, the Slavic gunman strolled out from around a metal storage container. The red tip of his cigarette was a bright spot against the shadows of his heavy brow and full beard. A Heckler & Koch MP-5, the weapon that had supplanted the Uzi as the world's most common submachine gun, hung from a shoulder strap. Hidden in shadow, Bolan watched the man walk up to the railing and take a last drag off his cigarette. The sentry flicked the cigarette out and it flew in arc before falling into the cold, polluted water and extinguishing with a hiss.

The man spit after the cigarette butt, then turned from the ship's railing and leisurely strolled across the deck. Bolan unfolded from the shadow. His hands found the two-inch-thick weave of one of the vessel's mooring ropes and locked his grip on it as he swung out over the water.

Like a kid on a set of monkey bars, Bolan swung hand-over-hand out about a yard or so, then lifted up his legs so that his heels could lock around the rope. He went still for a moment, reducing the momentum of his actions, then began to climb up the rope in an inchworm, accordion motion.

He worked hard, pulling himself rapidly up the rope to the gunwale. He slid over the edge and quickly drew the Beretta. He moved smoothly to the lee of the anchor windlass and crouched in its blocky shadow.

Bolan surveyed his surroundings. He ignored the cargo hold entrances in favor of the deckhouse. About a hundred feet of open deck separated him from the aft superstructure. He did not like the exposure and he had lost sight of the deck sentry.

Bolan scanned the dark but saw nothing. His ears detected the creaking of the mooring ropes and the gentle lap of waves on the hull beneath him. The Beretta was out and up and ready as he made his move.

He broke from the shadowed lee of the windlass, cut around the forward cargo hatch and sprinted toward the king post and crane assembly positioned between the holds. He dropped to one knee, Beretta up so that the suppressor was even with the hard plane of his cheekbone, his left hand resting on the cool metal of the deck. His heart bumped up against his sternum in a strong rhythm. His head swiveled on his neck like a gun turret, tracking for a target. His eyes narrowed in concentration.

Bolan heard the scrape of metal on striker and looked to his right. A lighter flared briefly in the gloomy dark as the sentry lit another cigarette from the starboard gunwale. Bolan extended his arm and leveled the Beretta. It was a long shot for a silenced weapon.

The pistol coughed once. The sentry crumpled, the cigarette tumbling from slack lips. The lighter fell and bounced off the deck, followed a heartbeat later by the corpse of the gunmen. Blood spilled out across the plate-metal flooring in a spreading stain of crimson.

Bolan slid along to the port side and reached the aft superstructure where he found a flight of stairs. He followed them to the bridge. The wheelhouse door was locked but through a grimy window he saw the glow coming from a wide array of sophisticated, modern navigational controls.

He crossed in front of the bridge and began checking doors. He was the consummate stalking predator, silent, deadly. He descend to the second deck on the starboard stair and found an unlocked galley door.

Bolan opened the heavy portal and stepped slowly inside.

The hallway interior was claustrophobically narrow and dark except for a single, dim emergency-light bulb set into the bulkhead at the far end of the corridor. Bolan moved carefully down the hall, trying doors and finding them unlocked.

Each room was a comfortable cabin, obviously designed for the ship's officers when the vessel was under way. Bolan found the first two clean, made up and empty. When he opened the third door, a bodyguard rose from his bed, the glossy pages of a European porno magazine sliding out of his hand. There was a submachine gun on the bedside shelf that was twin to the H&K MP-5 the other sentry had carried.

Bolan leveled his machine pistol and went to bark a warning, but the man was already in motion. The Executioner waited until the Serbian mercenary's hands found the weapon before pulling the trigger on his own.

The Beretta recoiled smoothly in his grip and blood splashed the twisted sheets beneath the bodyguard. There was a sharp wet sound as the 9 mm Parabellum rounds slapped into the man's flesh and pinned him to the bed.

Reflexively, Bolan put a third bullet into the man's forehead. The man lay still, and for a moment the only motion in the cabin was blood spilling from bullet wounds, then the Executioner was gone.

Bolan ducked through the metal frame of the cabin door and only had time to throw up one hand in surprise as the eight-pound head of a sledgehammer sailed toward his face. The man wielding the sledgehammer let out a snarl of effort.

Bolan's forearm caught the heavy tool on the haft just below the head of the maul. His arm exploded in pain and then went numb a heartbeat later.

He managed to deflect the killing strike but was driven backward under the force of the blow. He staggered up against the cabin doorjamb as the silenced Beretta went spinning across the deck. Bolan saw a wild-eyed man with skin like dull onyx bearing down on him in filthy jeans and a dirty flannel shirt.

The man lifted the sledgehammer and stepped in close to deliver another blow. The attacker's forearms and shoulders were thick with muscle and he was tall enough to see eye-to-eye with the six-foot-plus Bolan. His face was covered in stubble and his big, square teeth were stained nicotine-yellow.

Bolan lashed out with his left hand as the man swung the sledgehammer back over his shoulder. Bolan's thumb caught him square in the eye and the man hissed with pain and tried to shake his head clear, but Bolan felt the peeled-grape texture of the eyeball squish under the flat plane of his thumb and knew he'd hurt the man.

Bolan flexed the muscles of his back in the next instant and rebounded off the door frame and centered on his feet. Even as he repositioned, his left hand was drawing back and then lashing forward. His thumb targeted the man's neck adjacent to his Adam's apple.

The blinded sailor suddenly gagged and his face distorted against the sudden bruising. Bolan darted in and used his left hand to grasp the heavy maul by its handle. He locked his grip around it like a carpenter's vise and then slammed his forehead into the man's face. Bolan mashed the man's nose flat and smeared it across his face.

The man buckled at the knees and toppled, leaving the

sledgehammer firmly in Bolan's grip. As he dropped, the soldier jerked his leg up and drove his knee into the falling man's jaw.

Bolan struck at precisely the correct angle, and there was a sickening sound as the mandible separated from the skull at the hinge joint. The man slipped down to the floor and lay in a heap of slack, twisted limbs.

Bolan set down the sledgehammer and retrieved his pistol. His heart was pounding in his ribs from adrenaline, and his arm was throbbing with an agonizing pain that put his teeth on edge. Holding his pistol in his left hand, he forced himself to work his right hand, wiggling each finger and making a fist to ensure the bones of his forearm had not been cracked by the heavy blow.

The hand was weak and he knew his forearm would be black with a sheath of contusion markings, but he didn't think the bone had been more than bruised. He held the injured limb down by his waist and continued moving forward, weapon in his left hand now.

He hurried down the hallway to the final door on the deck. He couldn't imagine Taterczynski staying in any of the smaller rooms belowdecks designed for the regular crewmen. From the position of the doorway Bolan realized the cabin he stood in front of occupied a corner area, making it larger than the officers' quarters he'd just investigated.

He put out his injured hand and grasped the doorknob.

8

The President of the United States looked up from the report he held in his hand. His mouth formed a tight line, and his eyes were bright points in a dour face. He carefully set down the National Intelligence Estimate and scanned the pensive faces seated before his desk in the Oval Office.

Finally he settled on the director of the State Department's Bureau of Intelligence and Research. The INR had been the only intelligence-gathering agency exonerated by the exhaustive 9/11 Commission's report. Out of the sixteen U.S. intelligence agencies, the INR was the one that got it right the most often.

"Your people concur?" the President asked the INR director.

The gray-haired man nodded. "Absolutely. I'd tell you it was a slam dunk, but I don't want to jinx it."

Looking tired, the President sat back in his chair. He removed his reading glasses and rubbed his eyes as he slowly exhaled. When he was done he sat there, looking at the brief on his desk as if it had betrayed him personally. Finally he looked up.

"The Israelis know, of course."

It was a statement, not a question and no one bothered to answer the obvious.

"It won't stand," the national security adviser said quietly. "We already knew this. Tehran with a nuke is a deal breaker for them. What we would or wouldn't do is immaterial. Defense

Intelligence Agency reports that Israel began prepping bombers as soon as those Iranian jackasses moved the package down the highway under every military satellite in the stratosphere."

"So Tel Aviv's going to want us to live up to our end of the bargain," the President said.

No one answered him again. It wasn't a question. War, again, had reared one of its many ugly hydra heads.

"String the fleet along the Gulf of Oman from Karachi to Muscat. Mobilize armor and mechanized forces in Afghanistan and Iraq to reinforce security activities along the Iranian borders there," the defense secretary said, speaking for the first time.

"What about the Caspian?" the President asked.

The defense secretary shook his head. "Their 1924 treaty with the Soviet Union left them underpowered there, with no naval bases on the Caspian coast. Our air elements in Turkey should be enough to seal the ports."

"If—when," the national security adviser corrected himself, "the Israelis take out the threat they'll have to pass over U.S.-controlled airspace. Iranian forces will fire on our assets in retaliation. We have NSA transcripts confirming that. What do you want us to do?"

The President looked up. "I won't send men into harm's way, then ask them not to defend themselves."

"You understand, of course, where that will leave us," the secretary of state prompted, speaking for the first time since the meeting had started. Her voice was quiet.

The President nodded. He pushed away the thought

"When the Iranians fire, we fire back."

"Maybe there's another way," Hal Brognola said.

"Another way?" a skeptical President asked.

"Maybe. My man in Sarajevo, on that matter we discussed,

may be getting his hands on something important in a matter of minutes."

"For all of our sakes," the secretary of state said, "I hope that's true."

THE DOOR HANDLE TURNED easily under Bolan's grip and he pushed the door open, following close in behind it. He stepped across the threshold and into a lavishly decorated space taking up twice the square footage of the other cabins he'd investigated.

The room was dark as he stepped in and moved quickly to one side to avoid silhouetting himself in the entrance. A pool of stark light illuminated the far side of the room, revealing a lamp on an old-fashioned desk of deep walnut grain. Bolan looked at the man sitting there. Looking tired and old, Peter Taterczynski stared at him from a plush wingback chair.

The ceiling of the room was high enough to allow for a fan, and one turned lazily overhead. The room was thick with shadows but obviously ornately decorated. Bolan risked a quick look to ensure he was alone with the American traitor while making sure the man's hands remained flat on the desk.

"Your men are dead," Bolan said without preamble. "It is time now for you to answer for your crimes."

"How noble." Taterczynski smirked, but the smirk was tired and his voice held a tremble.

"Rise slowly and put your hands on the wall behind you," Bolan instructed.

Bolan moved forward several steps. He had cornered dangerous men numerous times before in the past. When faced with the reckoning for what they had wrought, many of the men had chosen a last desperate attempt at escape. Bolan was keyed to such a gambit now while his willpower alone suppressed the lightning bolts of pain from his injured forearm.

The former intelligence analyst made no move to follow Bolan's orders. His hands remained motionless on the desk. Beside him was a bottle of vodka and a water glass half filled with the alcohol.

"I said get up," Bolan repeated.

Taterczynski smiled. He lifted the glass to his lips and gulped half the contents, then carefully set his glass on the smooth grain of the expensive desk.

"Are you a killer?" he asked.

"Yes," Bolan answered.

"I can't go back. I can't stand the humiliation. I'm too old, too sick now to go to prison."

"Things you should have considered before you betrayed your nation," Bolan countered.

"True."

The man's hair was lank and gray in the harsh light. He met Bolan's eyes with his own, and the bags under them were heavy. Despite his wealth, it was obvious that life as a fugitive had not agreed with the former government agent.

"I can't go back," the old man said.

"I'm taking you back." Bolan looked down at him.

"Are you a religious man?"

"Religious enough."

"I was—still am, I guess—a Catholic. I thought I had cynically put such things behind me in my youth. But now that I am old and ashamed I find myself no longer quite so certain."

"What is your point?"

"That I can't kill myself. It's a sin and my soul is already so stained by my actions I fear receiving forgiveness now that I'm so close to seeing the Almighty."

"I don't have time for this crap," Bolan snapped. " I'm not going to kill you when you hold so much information. You can live a life of repentance in prison. I'm not here to offer mercy. I'm not here to judge you—your actions judged you, but I am your judgment."

"I told you I can't go to prison. I can't commit suicide. You must kill me."

"I won't shoot an old man just to release him from his own cowardice."

"I'll pay for my life."

"What?" Bolan demanded.

He was put off by the turn of events he had discovered on this ship. He was a past master at reading the intentions and sincerity of people. It was a prerequisite skill for survival in his world, and he had survived for a very long time in that world. Taterczynski was sincere, but about what Bolan still had not figured out.

"I was prepared for you," the man answered. "I put something of value on a flash drive, but I encrypted it. Let me show you."

Bolan suddenly remembered what Brognola had told him over the phone as he moved from Palermo into Sarajevo. "The Iranian connection?"

Taterczynski smiled and nodded.

"Move slowly," Bolan said.

Carefully, with a hand shaking from palsy, Taterczynski opened a drawer on his desk. He reached in and pulled out a flash drive.

Bolan caught a glimpse of a Walther PPK inside the drawer from where Taterczynski had removed the flash drive before the old man pushed it closed again. The traitor carefully set the flash drive on the desktop between himself and Bolan.

"What's this?"

"The price of my release. Including the Iranian connection."

"I could just take it, along with you," Bolan pointed out.

"It's encrypted with a binary box trap. Try to open it without the code, and it'll scramble into incomprehensible zeros and ones."

"Then we'll get the code from you."

"Time. What is on that flash drive is time sensitive. Open it in time and you'll have an intelligence coup that could save lives, perhaps as many lives as I've destroyed in my hubris. Take too long and the window closes."

Bolan looked into the man's eyes, read the truth there. "Give me the code," he said.

"Give me my release. It is the only thing I ask."

"What is the code?"

"Give me your word."

"How do you know I'll keep it once you give me the code?" Bolan countered.

"Faith is all I have left. Give me your word and I'll give you the code."

The Executioner looked at the traitor. He nodded once.

Taterczynski picked up a burgundy-colored pen from the desk and quickly jotted a series of numbers on a blank sheet of creamy paper. Bolan looked down at the numbers.

The old man looked back up at him. "This is the combination to the safe set behind the Monet on the wall over there. Inside you will find a hundred-dollar bill in an envelope. The code to the binary trap on the flash drive is the serial number on that bill."

Bolan looked at the former analyst. The man looked back at him. Tears made his eyes look weak and shiny in the unforgiving brightness of the lamp. His neck shook with his suppressed emotion.

"*Please*," the man whispered.

The Executioner lifted the Beretta and gave him his final freedom.

9

Mack Bolan sat in the War Room at Stony Man Farm. At the conference table with him were Hal Brognola, Stony Man's director, and the Farm's mission controller, Barbara Price.

The big Fed and the former NSA officer watched the phone set in the middle of the table. Bolan formed a steeple with his fingers and leaned forward to respond to the speakerphone. A bit of white tape showed from the end of his sleeve where the forearm had been bandaged.

"Yes, sir, I can understand your situation," Bolan replied. "I would be willing to help out, provided that this is a Stony Man operation. I'm getting too old to play with new friends."

"The DNI tells me that most of my usual assets are too occupied anyway, Striker," the President said. "As of late I've had to divert everything toward Iran not already tied up in other places in the Middle East. We need this done tomorrow, and we need replacement players. If we're going to get this done, we need you. Do it, and you and Hal will have earned my gratitude…again."

"I'll see to everything, Mr. President," Brognola answered.

"I trust you, Hal. Keep me informed. Thanks again, Striker."

"I'll do my best," Bolan answered, and the President hung up.

They sat in brooding silence for a few minutes, contemplating the task set before them.

Taterczynski's flash-drive information had been helpful,

but only a single brief on the memory stick had been truly critical. Of course the most vital piece of information had also been the most time sensitive.

In forty-eight hours at a resort in Mandalay Bay, Myanmar, the Association of Southeast Asian Nations would convene. ASEAN had first been created to form a bulwark against the spread of communism in the region, but as the cold war subsided Vietnam had been allowed to join the association on July 28, 1995.

The ASEAN meeting would be attended not only by high-level diplomatic functionaries from the respective nations, but also by their intelligence services. Industrial espionage, bribery and trade secrets were always high on the agenda at such gatherings, deep behind the scenes.

Vietnam would be participating in these discussions with a zeal and skill level unrivaled by their Southeast Asian counterparts. Part of their team would include a man named Andrei Lerekhov, a former KGB officer and now an adviser to the Vietnamese government.

Hal Brognola sighed. "Let's start at the beginning, go over it slowly and build a plan of attack from there. Barb?"

The honey-blond, mission controller oversaw Stony Man operations with skills both subtle and overt. She did not miss details, she did not fail to plan for contingences, she treated nothing as a "slam dunk" assessment.

"Andrei Lerekhov. The electronic intelligence expert is sixty-seven, a devoted Communist who fled to Hanoi during the glasnost years of Boris Yeltsin. He serves as a tech expert for their communications intelligence program in the TC2," Price began.

Bolan grunted in recognition. TC2 was the abbreviation for the Vietnamese Department of Military Intelligence. The agency had been around for quite a while but was believed to have really cemented its reputation during the Vietnamese occupation of Cambodia. Despite its designation as a Military Intelligence entity, its sphere of influence went well beyond military matters.

"More important for us than his code-cracking ability is his code-*writing* ability," Price continued. "Lerekhov could be the Rosetta stone of Vietnamese intelligence, which Washington believes has the most extensive files in the world, including names and account numbers for terrorist groups operating from the Pacific Rim to the Horn of Africa. Such information could turn the tide of the war against terror well into our favor in Asia."

"Why does a man who is such a devout Communist that he ran from an open Russia to a hard-line Vietnam suddenly want to defect?" Bolan asked. "And why put it out on the open market with an influence peddler like Taterczynski instead of coming directly to a sponsor agency like us or the French or Germans?"

"I think we may have a clue to the first part of your question, Mack," Brognola spoke up. "Carmen managed to dig something up out of the ether from our binary traps on the Vietnamese embassy in D.C." "Carmen" was Carmen Delahunt, former FBI agent recruited by Brognola to work with the Farm's cyberteam.

"Mr. Lerekhov put in a request to the senior official here to make contact with our State Department about arranging health care," Price explained. "It seems Andrei has cancer of the colon and intestines. And cancer of the blood. That request was denied."

"This was before we realized he had traded security codes for the software to Iran's nuclear program using Taterczynski as a middleman?"

"Yes, that was why he went back to Taterczynski," Price answered.

"So I go in, make contact and exfiltrate with the Russian," Bolan summed up.

"You get the Russian, we get the Iranian security software, hack and crash the system, avoid an Israeli-sponsored strike. Of course security will be tight. Beyond the official security about a dozen intelligence agencies from a handful of paranoid governments will be fielding bodyguards, security operatives and conducting surveillance taskings," the mission controller stated.

"That whole resort is going to be a rat's nest of bugs, counterbugs and so wired it'll seem like YouTube," Brognola added.

"Movement is going to be a nightmare," Bolan said.

"More than a nightmare," Price corrected. "Virtually impossible. Your only chance is going to be to fight fire with fire and, of course, as the President just pointed out, the NSA's field operatives are being run pretty ragged right now."

"Solution?" Bolan countered.

"There are other American assets in the region," Brognola said.

"We're going to set up a forward operating base in the resort to provide communications and electronic-warfare capabilities for your snatch," Price continued. "We'll be able to hack, to interdict and initiate systems security operations of hostile observers and give you the best overwatch and aggressive tech ability in that place. Our assets will deploy to the resort ahead of you and set up an on-site activities cell that will link Stony Man mainframes and sat feeds to your area of operations. They'll be responsible for getting the gear to Myanmar, through customs and into the hotel. They will stay in the background as tech support while you operate through the environment. When the snatch happens, they will disengage and leave the country by a different route than yourself and the target."

"Is this necessary?" Bolan asked. "You know I prefer to work alone."

"This time guns won't be enough, Mack," Brognola said. "You'll need the extra help to avoid being compromised— there are just too many observers in that location. Without someone to give you additional eyes and provide a smoke screen, you have no chance."

"What's their cover?"

"They will have press credentials. Cowboy and Bear have managed to camouflage a great deal of their gear as video cameras and recording equipment," Brognola answered.

"We'll need to take a look at the kind of assets, networks and stringers the U.S. has in play in Myanmar," Price interjected. "Ever since the military crackdown of 1988 they've been on our Human Rights Violation watch. They have massive corruption, a brutal regime and an ineffectual insurgency operating along the border with Thailand the CIA's been encouraging for two decades now."

"Let's start there," Bolan said.

Brognola nodded, then leaned forward and stabbed at the intercom button on the phone.

"Bear, can you join us in the War Room? We need to go over background data."

10

Bolan scanned the inaccessible mountain terrain of the Thai-Myanmar border. Inside the cockpit of the OH-6 Little Bird helicopter, Jack Grimaldi surveyed the night jungle below them through the heads-up display of his Forward Looking Infrared—FLIR—sensors.

The experienced pilot concentrated on his task while Mack Bolan sat beside him in the copilot's seat. Cloud cover was a low ceiling above them and the jungle formed an unbroken carpet beneath them.

"We're on-site according to GPS," Grimaldi said.

Bolan gave him a thumbs-up as the pilot slowed the Little Bird into a hover. They had taken off from a joint Thai military and U.S. DEA operation center serving as a base for monitoring opium activity in the Golden Triangle.

The Little Bird hovered and then, showing deft skill, Grimaldi slowly spun the light helicopter in a slow circle. As if by magic, the scar of an ancient road was visible through the jungle canopy.

"There," Bolan said.

The ace Stony Man pilot began to navigate the airspace above the almost completely overgrown road. Less than a minute later the ruins resolved from the darkness on the FLIR screen. Without hesitation Grimaldi lowered the helicopter into position.

Using a bottom-mounted camera and a laser range finder, Grimaldi gently eased his cargo down and released the rope connected to the pallet that dangled under the belly of the Little Bird. He lowered the nose of the helicopter and skimmed it forward.

"Good luck!" Grimaldi said as Bolan leaped from the helicopter and rappelled to the ground.

The old Buddhist temple was made from dark stone blocks more than a thousand years old. The rock walls surrounding the main building had crumbled, and creepers had grown up to choke the structure like the tentacles of some giant squid.

Above him Grimaldi climbed the OH-6 up to an observation overwatch height and backed off the area as Bolan walked toward a crumbling archway. On the cargo pallet behind him was a square of stacked wooden boxes.

Inside the boxes were Bolan's bribe.

The U.S. military had replaced the M-72 Light Antiarmor Weapon, or LAW rocket, with the M-136 AT4 antitank weapon. The result was that huge stockpiles of the 66 mm shoulder-fired, collapsible LAW remained warehoused around the world.

It required very little creative requisitioning on Hal Brognola's part to scrounge up a shipment of the older but still highly effective weapons to serve as both arming agent and bribe for Bolan's Myanmar alliance.

The Karen National Liberation Army, or the KNLA, was the military wing of the Karen National Union, a resistance group that had been fighting for independence from Myanmar's military junta since 1948.

After the "8888" popular uprising on August 8, 1988 ended in failure, the ruling body of Myanmar's junta, the State Peace and Development Council, or SPDC, had turned to China for help. In exchange for economic concessions, China had provided a massive influx of weapons and training that had led to the near annihilation of the KNLA.

The insurgent group had continued to maintain a toehold along the Myanmar-Thai border, but its operations had become more a matter of survival while the world largely ignored the longest ongoing struggle for independence in modern history.

Bolan was here to play ball.

In exchange for the militants' help, he would provide them with much needed direction and matériel, starting with the several hundred disposable LAW rocket launchers on the pallet behind him.

"Heads up," Grimaldi said over Bolan's earpiece. "I've got hot silhouettes on my FLIR. They're moving out of the wood line to your four o'clock. I'm picking up long weapons on every figure."

"Copy that," Bolan acknowledged.

He made no move to unlimber his weapons though he was suitably armed. If trouble came, Grimaldi with his minigun and rockets would make the difference. In the meantime Bolan's focus had to be on negotiating a favorable outcome if his plan was going to work.

He turned to face the direction Grimaldi had indicated, and after a moment caught sight of ghostly figures emerging from the deep shadows of the jungle. He assumed a nonaggressive posture and put his hands on his hips. The group of armed men in a motley collection of camouflage uniforms and tribal gear began to fan out and take up defensive positions along the perimeter of the ruins.

A comparatively tall figure emerged from the center of the deploying unit and walked toward Bolan. A stocky man armed with a saw and wearing a bloodred bandanna around his broad forehead followed the first figure.

Bolan blinked in surprise as the tall KNLA fighter drew closer. The man's hair was gray under a pristine Red Sox baseball hat. He wore upward of a dozen solid gold chains over a Red Sox jersey. His black jeans were tucked into U.S. Army issue jungle boots, and he carried an M-16/M-203 combination assault rifle and grenade launcher. As he approached, Bolan was able to see the man wore a gold earring with the Red Sox logo on it and had what looked to be either an exceptional knockoff or an authentic World Series ring on the middle finger of his left hand.

"You a Red Sox fan?" the man demanded in flawless clipped English. He reached out the hand with the jeweled ring on it and Bolan shook it. The man's grip was firm but not in an attempt to intimidate.

"I've always liked the Pirates," Bolan answered, nodding toward the man's baseball paraphernalia. "But I was as glad as anyone when they took the Series."

The guerrilla leader held Bolan's hand clasped in his own. He leaned in close and his other hand found Bolan's elbow so that he held the American in a sort of embrace. The man's eyes shone with the light of a zealot, even in the dimness of the jungle night.

"We have been fighting the bastards of the SPDC since 1948," he whispered, his voice tight with emotion. "When the Red Sox won the Series after *eighty-six* years I knew. I knew it was a sign that if we just endeavored to persevere we would triumph as well."

Gently Bolan extricated himself from the insurgent leader's enthusiastic grasp. He could feel the sincerity of the man's beliefs rolling off him in almost tangible waves. Bolan patted the man on his shoulder.

"I have brought you a gift that will help with that. Together, my friend, we will bloody the nose of the SPDC and embarrass them before the world."

"My name is Smith Dun," the man said. "I am a great warrior and a brilliant leader. In my youth I was a heroic pitcher with a very good fastball. If those are the weapons you promised, then we will do as you say and strike out against the junta that has imprisoned my country!"

Well, Bolan thought as he shook the man's hand again, he gets an A for enthusiasm.

Smith Dun moved toward the pallet and Bolan followed him. The night was muggy, and Bolan could feel sweat gathering under his armpits and at the small of his back. Mosquitoes buzzed in an annoying cloud around his face, and the smell of rotting vegetation was strong in his nose.

Out in the jungle a monkey screamed in primal outrage. Bolan could see more KNLA fighters emerging from the shadows of the jungle trees and taking up positions among the mounds of temple rubble.

Smith Dun stopped in front of the pallet of rectangular crates. He drew a long, flat-bladed fighting knife from his belt beneath the Red Sox jersey and used it like a pry bar. The nails in the pine wood that housed the LAW rockets released their purchase without a struggle in the heavy humidity.

Dun threw the top of the first crate down and pushed the packing aside. He reached in and snatched up the OD-green collapsible tube launcher. He hefted it in his hands and Bolan could clearly see him smile.

"They are all here, friend?" the man asked.

"Every one," Bolan answered.

"You and I have made a bargain, then."

Dun turned back toward his platoon of men and whistled once sharply. His whistle was repeated from somewhere inside the wood line. Men began moving forward, hanging their weapons from the slings as they approached the heavily laden pallet.

"You got the heat signature of a deuce-and-a-half truck just came to life, about six hundred yards from your position," Grimaldi spoke into Bolan's earpiece.

Bolan reached up with a single finger and broke squelch by way of acknowledgment. Seconds later the throaty rumble of a truck's big engine emerged from the jungle. Within a minute Bolan saw the vehicle crawling up the deeply rutted road, lights off.

The surplus U.S. Army two-and-a-half-ton truck rolled into the open courtyard of the ancient temple, and the KNLA men opened the rear and began loading crates from the pallet into the truck bed with well-coordinated efficiency. Within minutes three-quarters of the pallet had been loaded into the truck, the men working only with ambient light the whole time.

"Heads up," Grimaldi suddenly said.

Of course, Bolan thought, his chest growing tight with apprehension. Nothing goes smoothly.

"Ask your man there if he's supposed to have two more trucks," Grimaldi continued.

Already knowing the answer, Bolan asked Smith Dun anyway. "My overwatch says we got two more vehicles rolling our way. That your people?"

Instantly Dun had his assault rifle off his shoulder. "No, it must be the Tatmadaw," he answered, using the Burmese word for their army.

"We've got problems," Grimaldi cut in again. "I just picked up a helicopter coming in—outline makes it look like a Huey!"

"Copy!" Bolan answered. "Do you think the bird has made you?"

"I don't think so. My FLIR is probably head-and-shoulders above anything the Myanmar might have purchased second-hand from the Chinese. If I drop down behind the temple now, I could catch an angle."

"Copy. We'll handle the trucks," Bolan replied. "Dun, keep most of the men loading the truck. Pull seven and have them follow us."

Dun looked at him for a moment, sizing up the American stranger, then nodded once. He barked orders out in rapid dialect and instantly seven wiry jungle fighters leaped to obey. Bolan jogged over toward pallet and began breaking a crate open.

"Have them arm themselves. Follow me," Bolan snapped.

Dun nodded once toward his fighters, and the eight Myanmar insurgents began mimicking the American's actions and opening the crates filled with the LAW rockets. He could hear the grumble and growl of the new trucks now, their engines different from the American-built power plant in the deuce-and-a-half.

He held up the LAW in his hand as the rhythmic beating of the new helicopter broke over the treetops and the Tatmadaw gunship came flying in. A searchlight hanging from its nose clicked on with blinding effect. Gunfire broke out along the periphery of the jungle clearing.

Working quickly, Bolan jerked the pin loose from the end caps on the rocket launcher. He turned the tube sideways, grasped it in both hands, snapped it open, then put it on his shoulder and armed it by pulling down the pin lever set on the top. The fingers of his right hand encircled the tube, steadying it on his shoulder so that they rode along the ridge of the trigger.

All around him the squad of KNLA fighters mimicked his actions with impressive efficiency. Within thirty seconds nine 66 mm rockets were primed and readied for use. Bolan turned and began to sprint toward the crumbled wall lining the courtyard of the temple.

Above him the Myanmar Tatmadaw gunship hooked hard

around the courtyard, the searchlight playing across the scrambling KNLA fighters. A loudspeaker burst to life, and a man began to scream orders in Burmese. Bolan looked up and saw the door gunner swing his machine gun around. Men on the ground began to fire at the hovering gunship, their weapons spitting yellow-orange bursts of flame.

Bolan sensed something behind him as he went to one knee with LAW rocket on his shoulder. He saw Grimaldi suddenly rise up out of the shadows of the ancient, ruined temple and shift the nose of the bird toward the larger Tatmadaw helicopter.

There was a flash from the Little Bird as the rocket pods engaged, and then the larger helicopter was a brilliant flash of flame and burning metal as it turned into a fireball above their heads.

Metal parts began to rain down, and helicopter fuel splashed in flaming arcs toward the ground. Waves of heat rolled into Bolan hard on the concussion of the initial explosion. The stink of burning fuel overwhelmed the stench of the jungle vegetation.

Bolan looked away, down the road toward the approaching troop trucks. The vehicles had braked to a complete stop as more Myanmar border guards spilled out of the back and began joining the first teams in laying down suppressive fire on the temple and KNLA fighters.

Bolan sighted down the length of the LAW launcher tube then yelled, "Fire!"

Smith Dun repeated the instruction to his men as Bolan depressed the firing stud on the collapsible launcher. He felt the weapon recoil smoothly across the muscles of his shoulder.

The 66 mm rocket leaped from the front of his launcher tube and spiraled toward the trucks in a burning contrail. Like a diving bird the rocket spun into the side of the deuce-and-a-half truck.

The warhead slammed into the vehicle and exploded. All around Bolan the other LAW rockets flared into life, and the night air was alive with flying rockets. In a wave the weapons slammed into the Tatmadaw assault force. Explosions erupted in rapid sequence, tripping the fuel tanks of the big trucks and shooting their twisted frames into the air. Bodies and parts of bodies pinwheeled across the burning background canvas. Geysers of dirt erupted and rained down, along with bits of broken weapons and personal equipment.

The mass use of shoulder rockets in volley formation had emerged out of the chaos of Iraq. Insurgents had utilized the technique there with old Soviet RPGs to devastating effect. Bolan had just been able to apply that knowledge in a starkly vivid lesson. He knew that when it came time for these guerrillas to go to work with him in the capital, they would apply the lesson with deadly efficiency.

"Up!" Bolan snarled.

He rose and pulled his .44 Magnum Desert Eagle from the holster on his hip. The weight of the big pistol felt good in his grip. Around him the ambush squad he'd assembled lifted up their weapons and began to follow him.

Bolan leaped forward and began to run across the open ground toward the burning hulks on the road. Flames lit up the night in garish relief and illuminated the Tatmadaw soldiers trying to reorganize themselves. He saw one man push himself up off the ground and he triggered his pistol.

The 240-grain boattail slug slammed into the man with devastating force. Blood splashed out of the man's chest, and the Myanmar soldier was thrown to the side by the impact.

Around Bolan the KNLA fighters began triggering their assault rifles.

It was a slaughter.

The ambush squad moved through the assault area with merciless skill, moping up the wounded and remaining army soldiers. Bolan surveyed the scene, a grim figure surrounded by the burned corpses of his enemy. Smoke and flame swirled around him as Grimaldi lowered the Little Bird into position.

Smith Dun, his Red Sox jersey still surprisingly pristine after the violent action, shook Bolan's hand and the big American slipped him an encryption-capable cell phone.

"I'll use this to coordinate with you. Don't use it for other communications until we're finished with our business in Yangon," he instructed.

The guerrilla nodded and slipped the folding phone away in a cargo pouch beneath his oversized shirt.

"I will see you in the capital in two days," the Myanmar insurgent said.

Bolan nodded and then turned and climbed aboard the waiting OH-6.

"Let's go," he told Grimaldi. "I've got a train to catch."

The Little Bird smoothly powered up out of the clearing, leaving the burning wreckage and scrambling rebel force behind them.

11

Time seemed to be collapsing around Stephen Caine. The clock glowed, showing 3:12 a.m.

Lying next to the clock was a dog-eared copy of Lawrence Block's *Such Men Are Dangerous*. Caine read the book like a monk worried a bible.

The promise went through his mind over and over. It was like a bit of song or a scrap of rhythm he couldn't excise from his head.

…protect my country from enemies both foreign and domestic…

He lay on his futon mattress and listened to the storm gathering outside on the horizon. His eyes watched the ceiling fan turning overhead and the Black Crows played on his CD deck, the volume turned down low.

The bedsheets were bunched up with his restless turning and the Xanax wasn't working. Under his pillow he could feel the hard L-shape of the Beretta 92-F. His naked flesh was sticky from his fear sweat, and his eyes were gummy from crying.

…protect my country from enemies both foreign and domestic…

A peal of thunder cracked outside, and a burst of rain struck the kitchen window like ball bearings. Caine sat up and his temples throbbed. The futon was low on the floor beside a cheap wooden nightstand. The nightstand didn't go with the futon, of course, but nothing in his studio loft went with anything else. Charisa had gotten everything that matched when she'd left. She'd even gotten Emma.

The scene was fresh in his mind. The airport at the end of his last visitation, the last visitation he was likely to get since Charisa and that asshole lawyer she was screwing were moving to Seattle and taking seven-year-old Emma with them.

Emma looking up at him, her eyes the same beautiful, rich shade of brown as her mother's. Wide and innocent and trusting, not unlike how her mother's had been in the beginning of the marriage. Emma still trusted him, still loved him. She wasn't aware yet of how much his capacity to screw up even the simplest of things had turned her little world on its ear.

Then he walked her to the security checkpoint and handed his last connection to reality over to his ex-wife and the smiling asshole who was her boyfriend.

Caine listened to the rain fall. The Santa Anas had come and gone, and now the rains were falling. He wished he could see the ocean. He looked over at the nightstand. The government letter forwarded to him from his father sat there under four or five empty beer bottles. He opened the drawer on the nightstand and pushed a little Glock 26 compact model pistol out of the way and picked up his bottle of Oxycotin. He'd gotten the painkillers from Stephanie.

He took two pills and washed them down with a swallow of warm beer from one of the bottles. Naked, he stood and looked around the studio apartment, feeling lethargic and down, but numbed.

The TV was alive with flashing images from CNN. The sound was muted and the President was on the screen, gesturing wildly from behind a podium. The country was at war.

Again. The ticker at the bottom of the screen ran a blurb about hostages and then about gas prices.

Caine didn't see it. His eyes narrowed to gun slits as he watched the President's silent motions. His chest began to hurt and his stomach clenched. The muscles on his jaw worked in vivid relief as he watched the man.

"I owe you," Caine mumbled.

His gaze slid from the TV screen to the work area he had set up beside the ratty couch. Thunder cracked, just overhead now, and a bolt of lightning lit up the room like a strobe light. Caine's jaw worked as his hands formed hard fists. He felt like crying with helpless, futile rage. But maybe not futile…

"I owe you," he told the President. "I owe you for so much."

His hate was tangible, palatable even. He could taste it lying thick in the back of his throat, choking him, making it harder to breathe. He remembered the old saying—all it took for evil to prosper was for good men to do nothing.

Caine forced his breathing to slow as he looked around the apartment at the power tools, the bucket of gas, the compound that unclogged drains, the steel washers, Ping-Pong balls and electrician's tape all lying there with lethal promise amid a tangled nest of stereo wires. He felt a smirk tug at the corner of his mouth beneath his beard stubble.

He thought about the government letter announcing Justin's death in Iraq, and his smile faded back into nothing. He turned his back on the President and walked into his narrow, cramped kitchenette. He absently scratched the faded ink of the tattoo in the middle on his left deltoid. It showed a black ribbon with a red 75th printed in the middle.

He moved around the dirty kitchen counter and passed a sink full of dirty dishes stacked like tombstones. He opened the freezer and moved aside the .45-caliber M1911 pistol. He pulled out a grungy plastic ice tray the color of kiddie blocks and dropped some cubes into a dirty water glass. He poured three fingers of tequila over the ice.

He sipped the drink and watched the rain smear the tiny window at the back of the kitchenette. The rain fell hard and the Black Crows sang about heroin-addicted girls talking to angels. The tequila was oily and smooth as it slipped down. Somewhere inside of him he wanted to cry again, but the tequila and the pills kept him disconnected and Caine was glad because his father had never approved of crying.

No, he reflected, the old man believed that when you got hurt you hurt back.

IN THE DREAMS Caine was back in Somalia.

Fresh into the battalions out of the Ranger indoctrination program, not even tabbed yet as his turn to go to the Ranger School hadn't cycled up yet when they'd been deployed to Mogadishu.

In his dream he was there again and the Black Hawks had been knocked down and his company had been fighting its way clear, one bloody block at a time. Night had fallen, and everyone was shot to shit and there were thousands of militia around the ruined house and everyone there knew they were going to die.

It just kept getting worse. The gunmen, knowing American reluctance to kill civilians, had started walking toward the Rangers' defensive position using the women and children as cover. Hundreds of them pushing forward, firing their Kalashnikov AKMs from under the arms of terrified teenage girls.

At first the American soldiers had tried to shoot around the human shields, like Old West heroes, but then there were too many militiamen and they were getting too close. Caine remembered the first one, couldn't escape the memory. She was clinging to her baby and obviously scared, but still shouting at the Ranger house in defiance and with every shuffling zombie step she took she brought the deadly enemy machine-gun fire closer. Behind her a militia thug fired at Caine's window with his AKM, putting rounds downrange indiscriminately. But he kept getting closer, just like the man next to him and the one next to *him* and on and on.

Caine felt his stomach drop like a stone as he realized what he had to do. Then he did it. His burst cut short the baby's crying and cracked the mother's chest like an ax through wood. The gunman stood there stunned as his human shield tumbled out of his arms. Caine put the next two 5.56 mm rounds low in the militiaman's gut, hoping he died slowly.

Then there was another militiaman pushing closer, and another one, and six more after that and a hundred piled up behind them. It was then that Caine found the psychological balance that, once tipped, allowed a soldier to do what he had to do to live, no matter the cost.

After that Caine shot everybody who came in front of his sights. And he lived.

12

Mack Bolan took his passport back from the Myanmar border guard. He was conscious of the presence of the briefcase at his feet. The uniformed man passed by him down the train aisle to look at the paperwork of the other passengers. When Bolan checked the blue booklet before he put it away, he discovered the fifty-dollar bill placed there was gone.

He looked out his window at the jungle encroaching onto the track along the border station. It was humid, but the passenger train had air conditioning in the first-class compartment. Outside, a bored border guard picked his nose while his other hand cradled the pistol grip of his AKM assault rifle.

Myanmar—officially the Union of Myanmar—was the largest country by geographical area in mainland Southeast Asia. Historically it was also known as Burma by many organizations and states. The country was controlled by a violently repressive military junta that allowed little room for political organizations and had outlawed many political parties and underground student organizations.

Consequently Myanmar's foreign relations, particularly with Western nations, had been strained. The United States had placed a ban on new investments by U.S. firms, an import ban and an arms embargo on the country, as well as freezing military assets in the United States because of the military regime's ongoing human-rights abuses, the ongoing detention

of Nobel Peace Prize recipient Aung San Suu Kyi and refusal
to honor the election results of the 1990 People's Party.

Bolan saw the guard he'd been forced to bribe exit the
train and stroll over to the soldier who'd been so studiously
picking his nose. As the train lurched forward and began to
pull away, the Executioner saw the second sentry hand the first
a cell phone. As he watched the man he'd bribed talking into
the phone, their eyes met through the glass and the soldier
turned away.

Bolan felt a sense of apprehension that he forced himself
to put behind him. His caution was normal in such a police
state, and at the moment there was little he could do about
anything. The train got up to speed and almost as quickly the
ride became very rough.

As a result of the military government oppression, Myanmar lacked adequate infrastructure. Goods traveled primarily
across the Myammar-Thai border, which was also where most
illegal drugs were exported, and along the Irrawaddy River.
Railroads like the one Bolan now traveled were old and rudimentary, with few upgrades since their construction in the
1800s. Highways were normally unpaved except in the major
cities. Energy shortages were common throughout the
country, including in the capital city of Yangon.

Perhaps because of this Myanmar was also the world's
second-largest producer of opium, accounting for eight percent of the entire world production, and was a major source
of narcotics, including amphetamines.

Inside the briefcase at Bolan's feet were four books by the
Myanmar author Maung Hsu. Inside each of the books were
hidden the account and transfer numbers to money held in the
World Bank internal operations funds.

TEN MINUTES AFTER CROSSING the border Bolan looked at the time on his wristwatch. As if on cue the door at the end of the train car opened and an Asian man in a cheap suit entered. He was short and slight of frame, even by the standards of Southeast Asia. His hair was gray at the temples and he carried a briefcase in one soft, well-manicured hand.

The scholarly-looking man made his way down the aisle toward Bolan and took a seat on the empty bench across from him. Bolan looked him over as the man leaned down and placed his briefcase on the floor directly across from the identical one beside Bolan's feet.

"I work for Aung San Suu Kyi," the man said.

Bolan nodded. "I support her struggle," he replied.

In Myanmar's 1990 parliamentary elections the National League for Democracy had won 392 out of 492 seats in a massive, overwhelming display of solidarity for freedom by the population of poor nation. The military junta had voided the election and maintained its stranglehold on power in country through the use of brute force.

Soon after the election and the subsequent crackdown, some of those elected representatives had fled arrests and formed the National Coalition Government of the Union of Burma to continue the struggle for democracy. The movement had both a public face and a covert one.

"So many dignitaries and important men have come to my country to take part in the ASEAN conference," the man said. "They make sounds about the lack of progress in human rights in Myanmar, but they do nothing of substance. Meanwhile our children work as slaves, people are trafficked like cattle and the government tortures and murders."

"No one can save the people but the people," Bolan replied. "All they need is the assistance of concerned benefactors."

"Those benefactors must offer tangible proof of their support if they are to see the fruit of their efforts," the man warned.

"Support is as specified," Bolan agreed.

The man leaned forward and picked up the briefcase at Bolan's feet. He left his own behind on the floor of the rocking train. He rose and looked down at Bolan, his face inscrutable.

"In two days the students and workers of Myanmar will gather before the indifferent dignitaries and diplomats at the Mandalay hotel. These things have a way of getting out of hand."

Bolan nodded once. "That is as it should be," he replied.

The man strolled away up the center aisle and disappeared through the door leading out of the train car. Bolan settled back into his seat and relaxed.

THE TRAIN ROLLED into the capital thirty minutes later and Bolan grabbed his carry-on and the briefcase left behind by his contact before disembarking onto the crowded station platform. The humidity instantly plastered his lightweight shirt to his skin, and he was drenched with perspiration. He stood out in the crowd, white and tall in a milling sea of shorter people and brown faces.

He listened to the staccato cacophony of the rapid-fire Asian langue being spoken around him, able to distinguish words and phrases and snatches of conversations. A line of chickens sat in wire cages against one wall next to pallets of burlap bags filled with rice and stamped with UN markings.

Bolan pushed his way through the crowd. Passing under a huge clock, he entered a short green-tiled hallway just off the main platform where grungy, numbered lockers of battered and dented stamped metal sat under the benevolent gaze of a bronze Buddha.

He pulled a key from his shirt pocket and crossed to a tall

locker bearing the same identification icon. He stuck the key in the lock, turned it and opened the door. Inside was a black nylon knapsack. Bolan reached into the locker and pulled it off the hook. The bag was heavy as he slid it over his shoulder. He found the weight comforting, evidence of the precisely measured Italian manufacturing he valued so much. Beretta made fine weapons.

He turned and immediately noted the Asian man watching him. The man puffed quickly on a cigarette, which he dropped to the floor when he caught Bolan's eye. He lifted the edge of his lightweight suit coat and quickly flashed Bolan the pistol secured under his armpit. The man closed his coat and gestured with his chin toward the grimy door to the rest room across the hall from the silent Buddha.

Bolan's battle senses were on high alert. He didn't know who the armed man was. The Asian certainly wasn't part of his operational instructions. He had been dealt a wild card minutes after making his insertion. Still, things changed and he couldn't very well leave a threat at his back as he went about making his connection.

Bolan moved toward the door of the public rest room.

Flies buzzed in an insistent cloud around him, thirsty for his sweat. He waved an impatient hand at them as he walked past the lounging man. The man scowled at him and pushed himself off the wall. Bolan looked around as he put out a hand to push open the rest room door. He spotted no other players hanging back in a security or overwatch position. It meant little. Perhaps he had missed the backup crew in the crowd.

Things had taken a wrong turn in Yangon.

Inside the rest room several men stood at the urinal built into the wall. A pair of teenage male prostitutes stood listlessly beside the doors to the stalls. They wore copious amounts of women's perfume that did little to cut through the room's acidic stench.

Bolan placed his heavy black knapsack on the wash sink and waited, hands stuffed casually in the pockets of his trousers. If this had been an official roust, he would have been yanked into a side office by uniformed men. This was something else.

The man who had showed Bolan his pistol followed him into the rest room. He flicked a freshly lit cigarette into the urinal gutter where it extinguished with a hiss. He barked some sharp orders and held up a leather wallet in a hand with nicotine-stained fingers and dirty fingernails.

Instantly the occupants of the rest room turned and filed out. The man pinched one of the young males on the cheek as the hollow-eyed youth filed passed. The possessive intimacy of the gesture angered Bolan. He kept his face expressionless.

The armed man waved away an elderly man trying to enter the rest room and closed the door. He turned the dead-bolt lock and twisted to face Bolan. The big American looked at him. The man smiled but his eyes were the dead, gray eyes of a shark.

"You have broken one of our laws," the man began.

Bolan didn't answer.

"You had irregularities in your paperwork crossing our border. You were also seen in conversation with an individual of dubious reputation. You gave the inspector a bribe, and he in turn paid out something to his sergeant."

"Yes," Bolan answered. He narrowed his eyes. "Corruption is a horrible thing."

"I will of course need to see your paperwork and identification."

"In the men's room?"

"I prefer to see identification documents printed on U.S. paper."

Bolan removed a hand from his trousers pocket. It contained a thick wad of money. There was ten thousand more in the knapsack for operational expenses. It was easier to make the little man before him go away with money than it would be to commit murder in a men's room at the train station.

Bolan held out several hundred dollars. Eagerly the man reached for it. Bolan pulled it away, leaving him grasping at air. The man scowled.

"How do I know you are an official just because you have a gun?"

The man spit a curse and yanked out his wallet. Inside was a government identification card. Bolan scrutinized it quickly and his heart began to beat faster. The man before him was not a police officer or customs official. He was a member of the Office of Military Affairs Security, the state organization charged with counterintelligence.

His mission was too delicate to come under the scrutiny of a corrupt intelligence agent. His time frame in Myanmar was short, the window of opportunity narrow. It was one thing to bribe a crooked policeman. It was another thing to enter into a relationship with a representative of the very group whose plans he was attempting to foil.

"How do I know this is the end of it?" Bolan asked. His left foot slid forward slightly. "How do I know that once I pay you I won't be paying someone else and someone else after them?"

The man's cannibal grin spread so wide it threatened to split his narrow skull.

"I'll be sticking close, keeping a *protective* eye out on you. If anyone comes near I'll use my influence to keep them away." His tongue, like a twisting pink worm, worked at a gold tooth. "You were a lucky man when you found such a guardian angel in me."

Bolan extended the money. The man reached for it. Just as the Asian's fingers brushed the folded bank notes Bolan let them tumble to the floor. The greedy official's eyes followed it, tracking it like a hawk.

The man's own greed had sealed his fate. Bolan struck. He dropped his right shoulder and formed a hook in the bend of his arm. He lunged forward, placing his right leg behind the knee of the other man's leg and twisted hard from his hips.

His bent arm clotheslined the startled agent around the neck. Bolan followed through on his savage twisting motion, simultaneously tripping him backward with his positioned leg and rolling the unbalanced man over the fulcrum of his own hip.

The agent flew into the air, his eyes wide with shock at the sudden violence of Bolan's movement. He hit the hard tile of the rest room floor like a sack of loose meat, and his head snapped into the ground as the air was driven from his lungs.

He lay, stunned for a moment and fighting against the smothering shroud of unconsciousness. Bolan did not hesitate. Standing over him like a medieval headsman, Bolan finished the altercation.

His left leg swept up in a crescent sweep until his foot was even with his chin, then he snapped the heel of that foot straight down in an ax drop. Bolan's heel caught the stunned Asian squarely in his throat and crushed the trachea and larynx. The man shook as if jolted by electricity, and his eyes nearly bugged from his head.

He made gagging noises through his ruined throat as his face grew purple. Bolan placed a big foot across the crushed structure and pressed downward with his two-hundred-plus pounds, cutting off the blood flow to the man's head and starving the man's brain of oxygen even more quickly than by crushing the windpipe.

The crooked agent's hands flew ineffectually to Bolan's shoe, but his fingers had no strength. The Executioner watched the dying man's face transition from bright purple to ashen gray, and then the eyes slid shut in defeat. The man shuddered once then lay still, his hands sliding off Bolan's shoes and flopping like fish on the grimy floor.

Bolan dropped to kneel beside the copse and, moving with a quick economy of motion, stripped the man of his weapon and identification and then reclaimed the wad of money he had used as a lure.

He pocketed those items then grasped the body firmly by the lapels and rose smoothly. He ducked under the rising corpse and shouldered the weight. He took two steps and crossed the rest room to unceremoniously plop the corpse on a toilet bowl. He locked the stall door then climbed out of the narrow space over the divider.

He went to the mirror, washed his hands and fixed his hair and adjusted the fit of his clothes. He looked at himself in the mirror. His face was expressionless. Turning, he picked up his knapsack and crossed the floor and unlocked the rest room door. He moved through and out into the train station again.

He looked down at the hollow eyes of the male prostitute, who returned his gaze calmly, his face expressionless. Bolan remembered the possessive caress of the government agent on the youth's face, and his stomach tightened into an angry knot.

He felt overwhelmed for a moment, powerless and impotent in the face of all-pervasive and seemingly omnipotent evil. He couldn't save this youth, or thousands more just like him across the world; it was simply impossible. That was the truth, as undeniable as it was merciless.

But it didn't mean he wasn't going to try.

Bolan pulled the money from his pocket and held it out. The youth took the money automatically. It was a lot of money for a street urchin in a Third World country where the annual per capita income was just under 450 U.S. dollars. It was enough to change his life.

Maybe.

"Take it," Bolan said. "Take it and go. Get away from here. Now."

The youth nodded, though Bolan had no way of telling if he truly understood his words. The young man turned and took his friend by the hand and pulled him into the crowd.

Men began to push past Bolan and into the rest room. The rhythm of the platform at the Yangon station remained unchanged in its frantic pace. There was no blood to betray the killing, no smell of cordite on the air. People minded their own business in Yangon.

Bolan began cutting his way through the crowd. His hands found the face of his wristwatch. He was still on schedule and had plenty of time to make his meet. Standing head and shoulders above the milling people, he pushed his way through the crowd and out of the building where he hailed a cab. He gave the address to the Mandalay Resort and settled down into the back seat as the driver navigated the chaotic streets.

The streets were lined with people and the lanes jammed with rickshaws, bicycles, tiny passenger cars, mopeds and delivery trucks. Caucasian faces were uncommon, and there was a ready mixture of peasant garb and business suits. At intersections and in front of important buildings military police armed with long wooden batons and AKM assault rifles eyed the pushing crowds with bored faces and reflexive suspicion.

In the rearview mirror the cabdriver's eyes, yellowed and bloodshot, flicked up and the unshaved man regarded Bolan.

"English?" the driver asked, his voice heavily accented.

"American," Bolan answered.

"Ah, good. First time in Yangon?" he asked.

"Yep," Bolan answered.

"Welcome to Myanmar," the driver said.

13

Stephanie worked on Caine with the mechanical intensity of a locomotive piston. He looked down at her and saw the top of her head bobbing in a smooth, professional rhythm. He felt every nerve alive through his body, and he sucked in air through clenched teeth and squeezed his eyes tight shut while she worked in his lap.

His mind screamed at him to hold on, and he knew if he didn't think about something else quick he was going to spend his three hundred dollars in under three minutes. His mind spun like the wheels of an old-fashioned slot machine.

Stephanie took his mind off of what he had sworn to do, but his mind was never really off what he'd sworn to do. Maybe he thought Stephanie could save him. But no one on the outside could ever save a man from himself.

The presidential motorcade pattern was set. Caine knew there would be in the neighborhood of thirty vehicles. For his purposes his timing needed to be simple. Initial detonation would occur at vehicle number four followed by a secondary detonation at approximately cars nine or ten. This would put the presidential vehicle inside a tight kill box. If the explosion was large enough, the vehicles in the immediate vicinity of both target cars would blow, as well.

The main problem would be the electronic countermeasures placed in the lead car, the bomb-sweep vehicle. He had to—

Caine groaned deep in his chest as he lost control. Stephanie didn't miss a beat, and he felt the muscles of her throat working until he almost screamed out loud.

Stephanie locked her mouth in place as he shivered and calmed. Only when she was finished did she did raise her head. She touched the corner of her mouth where her lipstick had smeared. She seemed demure and poised. Caine's breath was as ragged as a running animal's.

"Can I use your bathroom?" she asked.

Caine could only nod in reply as he fought to gather himself. His mind was relaxed. The biggest factor was the bomb-sweep car. His plan would succeed or fail based on whether the first cache was noticed. If they missed the first one, it didn't matter if they discovered the second one; they'd already be in the kill box.

Which means the first device must be smaller, he reasoned. With cell-phone detonation codes he was susceptible to radio frequency jammers. The devices, called Warlock Green and Warlock Red, intercepted the signals sent from remote trigger locations to the IED, instructing it to detonate. The Warlocks prevented the signal from making contact. Without connection there was no detonation; the call was initiated but it was never received.

Despite that, Warlocks were not golden panaceas, even the advanced models likely used by the U.S. Secret Service. You needed to find the right frequency in order to stop it, Caine realized. That could not be easy, not with all of those cell phones and garage door openers out there being used to trigger the IEDs.

And just like that Caine knew what he had to do: prepaid cell phones. The chance for interception was still possible, but reduced. Redundancy—he had to build redundancy into the system. Two cell phones. Two triggers. If one was blocked, if jammers were used, then he'd have a second opportunity. The chance that the Warlock-style jammers would select two separate prepaid frequencies seemed an acceptable risk.

It wasn't foolproof, but it was plausible.

LATER, LYING NEXT to Stephanie in the dark, he didn't feel so alone.

It was an illusion and Caine knew it, but it kept him from plunging fully into the abyss. He knew where he was headed, knew well the path he'd been on.

Maybe if Charisa hadn't left, things would be different. Hell, he *knew* that if Charisa hadn't left his life would be different. But then he'd done everything he could to drive Charisa away, and the truth was that if he'd wanted to keep her Mr. Esquire never would have had her, BMW or not.

Women hurt you and that was the truth, he realized. But then men hurt women, too. People hurt people until nothing was left of relationships but vindictive words and crushed emotions. In Mogadishu, to live he had killed, but to live with his killing Caine had pushed away everything he loved. He couldn't live with the decisions he'd made, so he pushed those closest to him away until he was left with nothing but a woman he didn't love and a future he couldn't avoid.

But the demagogue was different, wasn't it? He hadn't asked for that; he indeed had asked for just the opposite. Then someone he hadn't wanted as President had gone and made a bunch of decisions that had hurt him and those closest to him when he was already down. People didn't get to do that, shouldn't be allowed to do. People were dying—six a day, the TV voice told him—and now that son of a bitch in D.C. was making decisions that would get more people killed.

More people like Justin and Angel Ramos. Or decisions

Get FREE BOOKS and a FREE GIFT when you play the...

LAS VEGAS
GAME

Just scratch off the gold box with a coin. Then check below to see the gifts you get!

YES! I have scratched off the gold box. Please send me my **2 FREE BOOKS** and **FREE GIFT** for which I qualify. I understand that I am under no obligation to purchase any books as explained on the back of this card.

▼ DETACH AND MAIL CARD TODAY! ▼

366 ADL EVMJ

166 ADL EVMU
(GE-LV-09)

FIRST NAME

LAST NAME

ADDRESS

APT.#

CITY

STATE/PROV.

ZIP/POSTAL CODE

| 7 | 7 | 7 | **Worth TWO FREE BOOKS plus a FREE Gift!** |

Worth TWO FREE BOOKS!

TRY AGAIN!

Offer limited to one per household and not valid to current subscribers of Gold Eagle® books. All orders subject to approval. Please allow 4 to 6 weeks for delivery.

Your Privacy - Worldwide Library is committed to protecting your privacy. Our privacy policy is available online at www.eHarlequin.com or upon request from the Gold Eagle Reader Service. From time to time we make our lists of customers available to reputable third parties who may have a product or service of interest to you. If you would prefer for us not to share your name and address, please check here. ☐

The Gold Eagle Reader Service — Here's how it works:

Accepting your 2 free books and free gift (gift valued at approximately $5.00) places you under no obligation to buy anything. You may keep the books and gift and return the shipping statement marked "cancel." If you do not cancel, about a month later we'll send you 6 additional books and bill you just $31.94* — that's a savings of 15% off the cover price of all 6 books! And there's no extra charge for shipping! You may cancel at any time, but if you choose to continue, every other month we'll send you 6 more books, which you may either purchase at the discount price or return to us and cancel your subscription.

*Terms and prices subject to change without notice. Prices do not include applicable taxes. Sales tax applicable in N.Y. Canadian residents will be charged applicable provincial taxes and GST. Offer not valid in Quebec. Credit or debit balances in a customer's account(s) may be offset by any other outstanding balance owed by or to the customer. Offer available while quantities last.

If offer card is missing write to: Gold Eagle Reader Service, 3010 Walden Ave., P.O. Box 1867, Buffalo NY 14240-1867

BUSINESS REPLY MAIL
FIRST-CLASS MAIL   PERMIT NO. 717   BUFFALO, NY

POSTAGE WILL BE PAID BY ADDRESSEE

GOLD EAGLE READER SERVICE
3010 WALDEN AVE
PO BOX 1867
BUFFALO NY 14240-9952

NO POSTAGE
NECESSARY
IF MAILED
IN THE
UNITED STATES

that would leave the world filled with more people just like him and his father. Men who pushed away the women they loved and didn't know their own children.

The politician son of a bitch had been wrong and his mistakes set things into motion, and the man was wrong so many times he would have been fired out of any other job. Incompetence. Incompetence was negligence and negligence was criminal, but nobody was doing anything to stop it. The system hadn't worked, and the demagogue had slithered through the failure and people were just going to keep on dying.

Caine cared. He wanted to elevate himself. He wanted to elevate himself beyond the limitations of his own past decisions. A man was the sum of his mistakes as surely as he was the sum of his victories.

But the truth was one man with a gun could change the course of history.

It didn't have to be right to be right. Truth was often like that, clumsy with ideals and long on practical realities.

Caine spooned in closer to Stephanie, feeling her warmth and sucking it up like a salve for what ailed him. Isolation, loneliness, despair. In the back of his mind he knew it was a lie, bought and paid for. Seen in that light it wasn't even much of a lie. But it was all he had.

"Steph," he whispered.

"Hmm," she murmured.

She seemed pretty sedated, which meant she would be willing to let him talk. That was good because he needed to get around to what he was going to ask her in his own way. What he was about to say didn't just have to do with her; it had to do with his plan and he needed to hear his reasoning out loud.

He was stoned and knew his conversation would seem disjointed and nonlinear. That matched his frame of mind, however, and part of what he was paying for after all—though he liked to pretend he wasn't—was for Stephanie to listen.

"I want you to stay with me for a while. Not to work anymore. Let me pay you to stay with me."

"You got that kind of money?" Her voice was its usual soft slur. He didn't even notice anymore.

"Yeah. I will. I have a little now, but come tomorrow I'm going to start having a lot more, enough for you to stay here."

"Three grand a week," she said.

She didn't ask why, probably didn't want to know, or hadn't even thought to ask. Men wanted her. They always had, and they found enough to pay for it. She had reduced her relationships to that. It was enough for her and she didn't want it to be more than that, even if it could have been.

Caine sighed. He could hear in her voice that Stephanie didn't care why he wanted her, only that the price was paid. He'd been fooling himself, and he hadn't been careful about how he'd proposed the offer. His bruised feelings were his own fault, he decided. He felt desperate to excuse her.

Life was tough, and if he'd ever thought differently then he hadn't listened to his father.

"Shit rolls down hill," the old man had said over the phone when Caine had gotten the government letter, "but blood, blood flows up the chain of command."

Caine would take Stephanie, he decided, even if she was bought and paid for.

THE PRESIDENT LOOKED UP at the discreet knock on the door. He set down the casualty reports. He read them every day, though he hated it. The numbers kept him rooted. He had to be strong enough to make their sacrifice worth it.

"Come in," he said.

His press secretary entered the office. A thin, calm man with thick hair and an unflappable manner.

"I had an idea, thought it might work to our advantage."

The President leaned back in his chair and lifted his reading glasses up onto his forehead. "What about?"

"You know the Syrian foreign minister, al-Kassar, is coming next week to speak before the Senate Oversight Committee to protest our recent activities against Iran."

"Yes, I imagine our 'recent activities,' as you put it, have caused them some discomfort," the President noted.

"Well, al-Kassar is on record at a French university several months ago denying the Holocaust. Then he reiterated that opinion again for an interview with an English-language magazine."

"I'm falling out of my chair in shock," the President said.

"I think I may have found a way to kill two birds with one stone, sir. Embarrass and denounce al-Kassar, stealing his headlines while at the same time shoring up some drift from the Jewish American League."

The President sat forward, sharply interested. Voting demographics carried elections. In addition, active campaigning carried elections. Active campaigning in key voting demographics cost money. Money came from wealthy donors. JAL was all of those things wrapped up into a single tidy present. Embarrassing the Syrians would make for a very pretty bow on such a large present.

"Go ahead."

"The National Holocaust Museum is holding a fund-raiser the night before al-Kassar speaks. Topics include modern anti-Semite trends in international academia. With your presence at the event it'll get full coverage. We won't even

have to spoon-feed the comparison to al-Kassar to the press—
they'll just run with it."

The President eased back into his seat again and the press
secretary could tell he liked the idea. The President liked
synergy, believed in daisy-cutter chains of political thought,
acting always through a combination, never a single punch.
Since the aide to the secretary of state was already engaged
in quiet discussions with the al-Kassar delegation, the energy
created by such a public challenge of ideals and ideologies
could only help to make the Syrians, and the Iranians through
them, defensive.

"Set it up," the President ordered. "Then get Hal Brognola
on the horn."

The driver crossed the bridge over the Irrawaddy River and took the exit leading onto the island and its resort. The Mandalay Hotel Casino was located on the north end of the river between different sections of Yangon. Bolan noticed the presence of heavy security almost immediately.

His initial briefing had informed him that the hotel casino was a luxury resort with 125 rooms on nine floors, two conference halls booked solid for the ASEAN convention, two indoor restaurants, one outdoor poolside restaurant, three bars, a banquet hall and a shuttle bus service into the city, supplemented by limousines for more influential or privileged guests.

The taxicab pulled up on the semicircular driveway in front of the wide, palatial steps of carved stone set in front of the hotel's front doors. Even before he got out of the cab Bolan could see the security measures the Myanmar government had put in place for the ASEAN conference.

Armed Myanmar national police and army units patrolled the grounds. According to Barbara Price's intelligence estimate, for every uniformed security presence, there were two or even three plainclothes undercover police officers or internal-security agents. Beyond these Price had assured Bolan that he could count on at least one out of five of the hotel "guests" during the regional conference being an intelligence or security operative for their host nation.

Bolan paid the driver and took his own bags up the steps and through the entrance of the hotel. The lobby was a large open space, ornately decorated and accessorized as befitted an international destination of such caliber.

A lounge area with tables and chairs took up one side of the floor plan, balanced by numerous counters for various guest services. The main counter was flanked by lavatories with gilded patterns and bamboo plants beside the doors. People bustled about, and the conversation of patrons provided a loud background buzzing.

Bolan gave his name at the counter, took his key and was directed to the elevators after refusing the service of a bellman whom he tipped anyway to ease the rejection. Bolan rode up the elevator, key card in hand. If everything was proceeding to schedule then his contacts should already have set up their operation in the suite.

The hotel was crowded, and even without specific intelligence warnings Bolan would have been suspicious at the presence of so many fit, hard-eyed men. The resort was crawling with muscle for the ASEAN conference.

Bolan was in a lion's den.

The elevator stopped on the fifth floor. The Executioner stepped out into the hallway and immediately saw at least two doors with men standing guard outside them. He frowned as he gathered his luggage to himself. Unobtrusive movement was going to be nearly impossible in this sort of environment.

One wrong action and the entire place could become a deadly combat zone.

He began to walk down the hall. It was long and narrow, heavily ornate with gilded wallpaper and thick carpet. The men guarding the doors watched him with interest unimpeded by good manners. Bolan ignored them.

Bolan passed the sentries and walked up to his door. He inserted his key card, watched the indicator light shift from red to green and heard the electronically controlled lock cycle over with a well-oiled click. He turned the door handle and pushed inward.

The door opened two inches, then stopped short, bumping up against the inside safety latch. He grunted in surprise; the Stony Man team had alerted his contacts regarding his arrival.

"It's Cooper," he announced, using his code name.

"Hold on," a female voice said from inside the room.

Bolan caught a brief flash of a pretty redhead through the gap in the door before it was pushed shut from the inside. After a moment the door opened and Bolan stepped through the doorway into the foyer of the suite. Immediately the redhead shut the door behind him and threw the dead bolt.

Bolan looked around the room. It was a plush suite filled with modern amenities. A slender young man with dark hair and glasses sat at a desk with three open laptops on it. He nodded curtly at Bolan, then immediately began typing again.

"I'm Jill Benson," the redhead said. She pointed to the agent preoccupied with the laptop. "And that's Mitchell Sparks. Forgive his rudeness but we're a bit distracted…."

Bolan turned a questioning eye toward the agent, and when he did he saw the body lying on the floor.

"He was here when we checked in," the statuesque redhead stated.

"Don't we need to get rid of it in case of a setup?"

"I'm monitoring both hotel security and local police channels," Sparks said. "Even with the lag of it going through my translation software I have picked up nothing, including cellular or landline communications, indicating a call has been placed." He picked up two test tubes from the table and held them up. Inside the sealed containers Bolan could identify two pinpoint microphones. "We landed here and we're already in the shit."

Bolan frowned. "What about parabolic mikes pointed at the window?"

"I'm using a counter sound generator," Sparks replied.

Bolan frowned. "Say again."

"This is a beauty. They're used in industrial models in large factories to dampen the white noise of machinery. They work by producing sounds waves with peaks where ambient sound waves have valleys and vice versa, canceling the organic noise patterns."

"I knew there was a reason you guys were sent." He was impressed though not surprised that Stony Man had accessed such competent equipment and personnel on short notice. Bolan turned toward Benson. "What did the body tell you?"

"Well, I don't have any crime-scene gear with me," she replied, then paused. "It wasn't exactly what we prepped for."

"I imagine not," Bolan allowed. "Just give me your impression."

Benson nodded, her eyes serious. She was a composed, capable agent and the sight of the corpse hadn't rattled her, Bolan judged. It made him feel reassured that he could still keep his team on top of things.

He followed her to the body and listened as Benson provided details.

"Asian male, twenties. One hundred thirty-five, one hundred forty pounds. Medium height and build for his ethnicity and regional norms. The reddish-purple discoloration in the dependent areas of the corpse indicates we found him at least thirty minutes after death. But look."

The American agent knelt and lifted the man's hand by

his fingers. Bolan saw that they were unnaturally stiff. The skin of the dead man was ashen against the stark relief of Benson's hand.

"Rigor mortis in the extremities, indicating the body has been dead for at least two hours."

"How was he killed?" Bolan asked.

Benson let the hand drop unceremoniously. She reached out and snagged a finger on the man's collar and pulled it down. Red welts stood out in livid detail around the man's throat, and Bolan could easily spot the concave instability under the Adam's apple indicating the larynx had been crushed, more than likely by a garrote.

"Strangulation."

Benson nodded. "I'm working on the theory that he surprised whoever was planting those bugs Mitchell found when he swept the room."

"Then they left the body?"

"Time might have been a factor," Benson suggested. "There's no identification on the body. Whether he came in clean or was stripped after the murder, I have no idea. I took his prints and a face-shot to run back through your people to see if we get lucky."

"Any luck?"

"Not so far," she answered.

"That's not all of our problems," Sparks announced from his station.

Bolan looked up from the corpse to where Sparks worked his cybernetic magic. It was a testimony to Stony Man's expertise that they'd been able to slide the gear through customs masquerading as television camera and editing communications gear.

"What else we got?" Bolan demanded.

Sparks removed his glasses and sat back to look squarely at Bolan. "If we want our op to go off like planned in six hours, we'd better make some decisions. On the plus side both your professor and the Red Sox fan have reported they're in position."

"Show me what you've got," Bolan prompted as he rose from beside the corpse and crossed the room to stand next to Sparks. He was running through a list of contingency plans he'd made while conceiving the operation. Finding a corpse in his hotel room hadn't been one of them.

"I've tapped into the hotel's communications switchboard through our telephone line. I simply followed the signals to allow me to access the closed-circuit television system, the landline and alarm network. That part was easy. The hard part was not alerting all the other taps I already found in place there.

"This is a van Eck monitor." Sparks pointed at one of his open laptop screens. The laptop was attached to a small electronics box outfitted with an antenna similar to the one used on sat phones. "Computer equipment, especially monitors, emit radio waves when in use. I can intercept these signals and recover the data displayed on the screen. It's entirely passive and unde-tectable and reliable out to a range of three hundred yards."

"If we can do it, can't they do it to us?"

"I'm using fourth-generation TEMPEST gear," Sparks replied. "It was sent over through Justice via some contacts in the NSA. I'm also using the countersound generator."

"Is that why it sounds slightly tinny in here?" Bolan asked.

Sparks nodded. "Yeah, this hotel is a flipping cesspool of listening devices, so I'm running it kind of rich. But here's our problem." The tech whiz pointed toward one screen. "Our target has a hit team here for him."

"What?" Bolan snarled.

"I snatched some IMs being traded on a laptop near our

room. It included some dates and conference times that correspond with our boy, so I got suspicious and ran it through my translator software. Chinese intelligence is apparently a little miffed."

"Miffed enough to murder a Vietnamese agent?"

"Since the border war in the early 1980s, things have remained strained," Sparks pointed out. "An ex-Soviet technology expert butting his nose into signal communications operations along that disputed border is probably the last thing Tiananmen Square wants."

"They put up with it for a while," Bolan pointed out. "Lerekhov's been in Vietnam for some time."

"I don't have all the answers," Sparks admitted. "All I know is that in a hotel room very close to us there's a team of Chinese government hitters here to put the squash on our target."

"Sometimes why isn't important—just knowing you have to act is enough," Bolan muttered.

"Speaking of that," Jill Benson broke in, "how do you want to handle our guest?"

Bolan nodded toward the redhead, then turned back to Mitchell Sparks. "Give me something to figure out a plan to pinpoint the location of the Chinese team," he said. "Just get me a name, a room number, a floor, hell, a compass direction if that's all you can manage."

Sparks nodded and turned back to scrutinize his computer screens. Bolan crossed the room to the cadaver and squatted by the dead man's shoulders. He jerked his chin toward Benson.

"Grab his legs," he said. "We'll move him onto the bed for now."

Immediately the redhead moved to help Bolan. Together they rose and lifted the man onto the bed. Bolan quickly scanned the carpet where the man had lain to see if any blood or other bodily fluids had made a stain. As far as he could tell with a cursory inspection, there was nothing.

"We can't keep him here," Bolan said.

"I know," Benson admitted. Her voice was steady but Bolan could tell by the strained look around her eyes that she wasn't happy at the prospect of dealing with a corpse.

"I can do it," he offered.

Benson shook her head. "Mitchell's doing his magic. You're going to need to do a reconnaissance. It makes the most sense for me to take care of disposal. I'll wrap him up before he's too stiff, then get some locals to pose as maintenance staff and cast the body out. I'll get the necessary uniforms and talk to my contacts later, but first I need you to get me rope and tape," the calm redhead told Bolan.

"I'll get the tape from the gift shop. There's rope and a knife in my equipment package in the knapsack." Bolan nodded. "Let's get started, then."

BOLAN STEPPED OUT of the hotel room and into the hallway, closing the door carefully behind him. He looked up and down the hall, placing the bodyguards he'd seen earlier. He straightened his shirt and smoothed down the front before casually starting for the elevators. He felt the sentries' gazes on him as he passed them.

Surreptitiously he inventoried the hard-faced men as he passed them. He had to admit to himself that it would be impossible to identify the men's ethnicity. Even if he had been able to spot them as Chinese, it was no guarantee they were the ones sent to kill his target. Bolan wasn't about to gun down a party of government bureaucrats just to be safe.

When he struck—and as he entered the elevator he knew that without a doubt he would have to strike—he would be absolutely sure of his target. As the elevator started down, Mitchell Sparks's voice bled into his ear through the Bluetooth he had set to walkie-talkie mode.

"I'm up, and I can see you," Sparks said. "There are CCTV cameras in the elevators but not the landings or halls. I'm hooked in passive to the video feeds, so I can cruise through the system and receive the images, but if I try to cut a feed or control a camera I'll give the surveillance crew evidence that I'm there."

"Can you zoom and pan if I need?" Bolan asked.

"Yes. I can freeze the images on my screen then toy with them from my console, not from the camera. If something bad happens I can hijack controls until they run a diagnostic and spot the hack. They'll know someone has jumped the system but not from where."

"Audio?"

"I've hooked into the resort security comm channels. It feeds into a dedicated laptop with a transcription and translation program. I can see it scrolling down in English as they talk back and forth."

"I'm glad you're here, wizard," Bolan said.

"Don't make me blush," Sparks replied.

"You be ready to ditch and run if I give the word," Bolan warned. "When the deal goes down, I need to know you and Jill are headed toward safety."

Bolan signed off just as the elevator doors slid open in the lobby, which was just as crowded as it had been earlier. He moved through the crowd toward the gift shop. There were more Occidentals at the resort than there had been at the train station, and he didn't feel as if he stood out quite so much. Hopefully he'd been mistaken for a reporter covering the ASEAN conference; there seemed plenty of them.

There were also plenty of fit-looking men wearing suit coats and blank expressions, he noticed. In the gift shop he used a clean Visa card to purchase two rolls of clear tape.

He turned to head back upstairs to their suite when things began to go wrong.

15

Caine entered his apartment. His knuckles were scraped raw, and his shirt was splattered with blood. In one hand he carried a gym bag filled with money. A lot of money. It was the third such bag he had been able to obtain working as a collector for a local criminal network that welcomed the skills of disenchanted Rangers.

He entered the kitchen and saw Stephanie standing over by the counter next to his computer.

"Hey, Steph."

She looked up at him, her face expressionless. Her eyes were glassy. She had a small pile of cocaine on a makeup compact sitting next to her.

"Hey, sugar, how'd it go?"

He could tell by the distracted air of her voice that it wasn't really a question because she didn't really care about the answer. He answered anyway. He was paying dearly for the charade.

"It goes like it always does," he said. "Heads get cracked, money gets made and nobody goes to the police because everybody is dirty."

Stephanie snorted a bump off the compact mirror by way of reply. She was standing in heels and lingerie. It was an obvious, even ostentatious display. It lacked class and was all the more effective for it. One didn't have to approve of getting hit by a baseball bat for it to hurt.

To see Stephanie was to want her. She smelled like lavender and Caine felt a tug in his crotch, a reptile-brain response hardwired to respond to large eyes, full lips, heavy breasts and the smooth curve of a feminine ass, whether it was wise or correct or proper or tasteful.

He unbuttoned his shirt and went to the bathroom sink, where he left the door open. He stripped down to his waist and began to try to scrub the bloodstains out of his shirt.

"Why do you do that?" Stephanie asked.

He looked up and saw her leaning in the doorway. Her bra was crimson and her French-cut underwear was the same color above sheer, thigh-high stockings. She was impersonally beautiful, like a painting locked behind glass.

"What do you mean?" he asked.

"I mean just throw the shirt away, Caine. It's ruined. Buy another one. You can more than afford it. Christ, how much cash you got already?"

"Enough to keep you." He carefully scrubbed at the bloodstains. It was important to clean up the blood. He didn't know why; it just was.

"You wanna fuck?"

Her eyes were heavy lidded and as bright as steel in the sun. Caine looked down at the bloody shirt. The water in the sink was hot and had turned pink. Blood red, money green, he thought. He looked up into his eyes in the mirror. His erection was apparent in the reflection.

He looked at Stephanie and she smirked at him. The sociopathic glint should have been enough to turn him off, but he wasn't wired that way. She turned like a dancer on four-inch heels and bent over slowly at the waist, like a cat arcing her back to a friendly hand.

The movement showed her sex and Caine's eyes unfocused slightly. He forgot about cleaning the shirt. He'd buy another. He undid his pants with one hand and moved forward.

LATER ON, while Stephanie did more drugs, Caine mentally reviewed the section he had read in a library book on psychology.

He evaluated the information and understood that he had evolved through the crucible of his experiences to an understanding above and beyond laws. He was sure of it. He acted in accordance with his own moral guideposts. In the end that was all anyone could do because everyone was alone. If Stephanie had taught him anything it was this. His moral guideposts dictated that he could kill the one to save the many.

It meant leaving Stephanie, but sacrifice accompanied commitment. The right thing to do was often the most painful.

He had enough money. It was time to marry motivation to opportunity. Time to stop fooling himself into thinking he wasn't going to get his payback.

He had a country and a generation to save. He just knew it.

16

"What are you doing?" Bolan asked Mitchell Sparks over his Bluetooth.

"What do you need?" the electronics specialist responded.

"I'm still in the lobby. Can you scroll and get me?"

"One second."

Sparks began a complicated dance with his mouse pad on one of his open laptops. He cut through several streaming-video pages and found the overview of the lobby. He jumped from one security camera to another until he had Bolan up on his screen. He double-clicked and brought up the picture.

"I got you," he said. Bolan stood next to a potted fern chatting into his Bluetooth like any number of foreign reporters and businessmen in the crowded lobby.

"Over my right shoulder is a group of Myanmar soldiers."

"Hold on." Sparks's fingers flew over the keyboard until the screen had isolated a group of three soldiers armed with AKS folding-stock carbines. The trio stood in an ornate alcove watching the milling crowd with bored expressions. The sophisticated software in his laptop zoomed right in on the passive feeds coming from the resort security cameras that he had hacked into using the landline in the hotel room.

"I've got 'em," he said quietly.

"The guy on the left," Bolan directed.

Dutifully, Sparks worked his tech magic and captured the man's face. "I have him."

"Good. I think that's the soldier who looked over my papers at the border crossing."

"Understood," Sparks noted. "Coincidences usually aren't."

"More than that," Bolan said. "What's his rank?"

"I'm familiar with military insignia but I'm not expert…" He adjusted the resolution on his screen. "Captain?"

"Good copy, that," Bolan acknowledged. "The guy was a private when he checked my passport and now he's a captain."

"Uh-oh," Sparks muttered. "I'm sending his picture stateside to see if I can get a positive ID, but for now I'd say avoid him."

"Great, his post is right by the elevators."

"If he were on to you specifically, wouldn't he just be raiding the room?"

"He's an unanswered question," Bolan acknowledged. "If I'm not at the front of his mind at the moment, I'd like to keep it that way for as long as possible."

Sparks turned in his seat and began typing on a second laptop. He pulled up the resort blueprint and began giving Bolan directions to circumvent the impromptu army checkpoint. Bolan grunted in response and began following his directions.

"By the way," Sparks told Bolan, "I'm getting Fox News feed here and a local station. It seems student protests are starting to gather steam."

"That's your tax dollars at work," Bolan answered.

His plan was simple, the way the best ones were. Increased crowd activity in the form of protest marches and perhaps even riots would force the security forces arrayed around and within the resort to turn their attention outward instead of inward. Not just outward, but outward to the west and the city side of the resort, away from the river edge to the east.

Following Sparks's directions, Bolan walked down a short hallway just off the main lobby that led away from the main elevator banks and toward one of the resort's many pools. He passed several guests and employees as he made his way down the carpeted corridor.

He opened a door set unobtrusively into the wall and entered a stairwell. Bolan moved up the stairs. On his way he passed a solemn-faced guard standing in front of one of the fire doors. His face was an impassive mask as Bolan walked passed him. The man was short and squat but with the neck and shoulders of a defensive back. His hair was short and parted on one side. There was silver at his temples, and his eyes were slanted slightly downward. His head swiveled to follow Bolan's progress, and Bolan spotted a tattoo of an Oriental ideogram along the thick neck muscle.

Bolan looked away and continued moving up the stairs, giving no indication of the sudden shock of recognition that had just created a starburst in his memory. At his floor he stepped through the heavy fire door and into the hallway. The two sentries posted outside the rooms there turned immediately in his direction. The one closer to Bolan let his right hand creep toward the inside of his suit jacket.

Bolan walked down the hall, his face nonchalant. The man recognized Bolan and slightly relaxed but kept the big Westerner under scrutiny. Bolan made it to his room and used his key card to unlock the door. Once inside he closed the door behind him and threw the dead bolt.

Mitchell Sparks looked up from his station. "Everything cool?" he asked.

"As cool as it can be," Bolan said.

He crossed to Sparks's desk, where he spotted a heavy, streamlined Mont Blanc pen next to a pad of vanilla writing sheets. Quickly Bolan sketched the tattoo he'd seen on the sentry's neck.

"That's not perfect," Bolan said. "But it should be close enough for you to find a match in the Interpol and Homeland Security databases, if it's there."

Sparks looked at the paper. "I'll run this through the image encyclopedia. Where'd you get it?"

"It was a tattoo on the neck of a hard case standing in front of the fire door to the floor two levels below us. The joker could have been Vietnamese, but that ideogram jogged something in my memory. It's just a hunch."

"Well," Sparks allowed, "this is a target-rich environment."

The young cyber specialist took Bolan's drawing and fed it into a scanner. Immediately it appeared on the screen of one of his laptops. He scrutinized it closely, his ubiquitous headphones dangling around his neck. Sparks had a strong background in kanji from personal interest, and he was able to immediately dismiss the ideogram as not coming from a Japanese lineage.

Bolan picked up the bag containing the tape from the gift shop and headed for the bedroom.

"Hey, Jill," he said as he entered the bedroom.

"Hey, Cooper," Benson answered.

She had wrapped the corpse tightly in the shower curtain. The bedclothes lay on the floor, ready to be wrapped around the body once the shower curtain was secured with tape.

Bolan handed her the tape, and together they worked quickly. Finished with the tape, they encased the body in the bedclothes.

"I'm going to hunt down some hotel staff uniforms," Benson said crisply, "and some people who'll whisk this out of here."

Bolan opened his mouth to offer his help but Benson

silenced him with a quick shake of her head. A tendril of red hair fell out from behind her ear and across her face. She used her hand to push impatiently back into place.

"You know it makes more sense for me to be the one," she said simply. "Besides, if something happens you have to be free to go after Lerekhov."

Bolan nodded and stepped back. They walked out into the hotel room and Benson made for the door.

There was a clatter of Sparks's fingers on his keyboard before he looked up. He turned his sharp chin and looked over his shoulder.

"Cooper, I got a match on that tat," he said.

"Good. Hold on," Bolan answered.

He turned toward Jill Benson and began to unlock the door to the room. "You have your Bluetooth?" he asked. "You need a pistol?"

Benson quickly patted her pockets but came up empty.

"My comm unit's over in my carry-on. Right there by the nightstand."

Bolan crossed the room and retrieved it for her. He handed it over and watched as she put it on and powered up the link.

"Pistol," he said.

"You think that's wise?" she countered. "I get busted with a pistol and it's over. I'm not getting in a shootout with cops to get away."

"What if the people who sent *him*—" Bolan pointed back to the bedroom "—decide to ask you some questions about how he got in that state? You get pinched, you go to plan B, dump and run, just maneuver till we can arrange extraction."

"This'll be a piece of cake," Benson said and offered a tight smile. "Back in a flash."

Bolan crossed the room and stood behind Sparks after

Benson closed the door. He looked down at the image of the tattoo he had drawn as it sat displayed on the laptop screen. A paragraph of text was located beneath the image.

"Vietnamese special forces?" He frowned.

"Not just special forces—naval commandos. The literal translation is 'Malevolent Frog-Dragon,'" Sparks specified.

"That seem like very good op-sec to you?" Bolan grunted.

"No, but it might not have been intended for covert action."

"What do you mean?"

"I mean the unit is a group of amphibious scout raiders for the Vietnamese naval infantry divisions. The unit isn't classified or secret any more than our Rangers are secret. A young guy serving in the battalions might get a Ranger Scroll tattoo and no one would say boo—it's not like getting a tattoo saying Combat Applications Group," Sparks explained, referencing the correct terminology for what was commonly called Delta Force. "Now if that Ranger goes on to work in something not overtly clandestine like undercover espionage but as a diplomatic security operator or a Secret Service agent, then you have no op-sec issues."

"Well, that would tend to eliminate him as a candidate for our hit squad," Bolan said. "That would make him, probably, a security team member for the official Vietnamese delegation."

"I agree," Sparks said. "But it gives us a place to start—two floors down."

JILL BENSON CLOSED the door to the hotel room and began to walk down the hall. The sentries in the hall watched her with impassive gazes and intrinsic suspicion. She ignored them.

She approached the elevator banks and pushed the button to call a car. After a brief wait one arrived and a bell dinged loudly as the gilded doors slid open. The car was filled with three men. Benson's heart leaped up into her throat, but she kept her face neutral and forced a distracted smile. All three men were dressed in the uniforms of Myanmar national police.

The men broke off their conversations and regarded her. Their eyes scrutinized her, taking in every detail. After a moment the youngest man nodded and stepped back to give her enough room to enter the elevator. His partner, an overweight fortysomething with an Elvis pompadour, pushed the button to keep the elevator door open.

Jill Benson swallowed a lump out of her throat, froze her smile in place and entered the elevator.

17

Caine had his bags packed and sitting by the door. The apartment was empty and silent.

Stephanie had left without arguing when Caine told her it was time to go. There had been a moment at the door when she'd paused, as if she'd wanted to say something. Caine had frozen then and felt his throat suddenly constrict in some unnamed, misunderstood emotion. But both of them had been too broken to make the first move, and in the end Stephanie had slipped out the door and closed it gently behind her. Caine had locked the door.

Caine wandered over and picked up his cell phone, dialing the number from memory. He sank onto the couch while the phone at the other end of the line rang. There was a familiar pressure in his chest and behind his eyes. Again, it was a presence he couldn't put a name to, not anymore. It was there but it hardly even hurt.

"Hello?" Charisa answered.

Caine could tell by the curt tone of his ex-wife's voice that she knew it was him. He closed his eyes and his tongue felt too thick to form words, as if it were some animal he couldn't control filling up his mouth, choking him.

"Hello?" Charisa repeated.

Caine opened his mouth. *I'm sorry,* he tried to say but he couldn't force the words out.

"Goddammit," she finally snapped, "I know it's you. I have caller ID. What are you doing?" She paused. "If you want to talk to Emma, you can just forget it. You should have called on her birthday. Jesus, you're such a dick."

Tears welled up in Caine's eyes and his mouth was working and his hands started shaking so badly he could barely hold on to the phone. Despite this he could not will the words out, couldn't force himself to say what he needed to say.

"Don't call back!" Charisa shouted.

There was the sound of rustling on the other end of the line and suddenly Mr. Esquire's voice was on the phone. His voice was calm and reasoned, a courtroom voice, but Caine could hear the strain of the man's fear as clear as church bells.

"Look, Caine," he said, "if you love Emma, if you give a damn at all about Charisa, you'll just leave us alone." The man drew a breath and when he released it he sounded almost as tired as Caine felt. "We're a family now. You…you had your chance. Just leave us alone."

The line went dead. So did Caine.

He hung up the phone and rose. He wandered into the bathroom and began shoving prescription pills into his shaving kit, then stuffed his shaving kit into the side pocket of his suitcase. His tears evaporated. He walked over to the apartment door and picked up the rest of his luggage.

He chewed a pill chosen at random from his pocket and began to feel better.

He'd always been good at grand gestures; it was the minutiae of daily living that continually tripped him up. But what was minutiae, anyway? One man with a gun could change history, and that was the truth.

Caine opened his door and walked into the hall. He didn't bother closing the door behind him.

18

Jill Benson turned her back to the men in the elevator and watched the doors slide closed. The enclosed space was deathly silent, and she could feel the weight of the three men's stares on her. It made her skin crawl.

She swallowed hard and forced herself to remain calm. Her wireless communicator was a comforting weight in her ear. The line was open, the circuit modified to be voice activated. It was the only bit of solace she had.

The elevator slid to a smooth stop two floors down, still way up above the main lobby. An Asian couple, the woman in an evening gown and the man in a well-fitting tuxedo, stepped forward to enter the elevator car.

From over Benson's shoulder one of the uniformed men held up a hand barring entry, and the couple stopped immediately. Their eyes went to Benson and they watched impassively as the doors closed.

The elevator started with a slight jerk.

There had been plenty of room in the elevator compartment for the couple, Benson realized. It could have been too crowded for one of the men, personally, though, she tried to reason. Everything was still fine. The hotel was crawling with security forces; it was hardly unlikely that she would find herself sharing an elevator with a group of policemen.

There was no way for them to suspect she had a corpse in her room.

The elevator slid down another two floors.

The man on her right leaned forward, reaching around her. He was close enough that she could smell what he'd had for lunch—*buk-sak,* fish paste mixed with rice and drenched in a hot Thai-style sauce. The officer brushed his arm past her shoulder as he pushed a floor button and then stood straight.

The elevator slid to a halt, the doors opened with the familiar, subdued ding. The landing was deserted. Benson made to step out of the way of the three men and let them exit the elevator.

Hard hands grabbed her under her arms and propelled her forward. The heel of someone's palm struck her in the back and she stumbled, almost falling and the hands on her arms tightened into vises.

"No!" she snapped. The wireless communicator was still in her ear. "I don't want to get off on floor number eight, I don't want to go with you!"

MITCHELL SPARKS CAME UP out of his chair like a jack-in-the-box on speed.

Bolan looked up, slightly startled.

"Jill just got nabbed!" Sparks said.

"Where was she?" Bolan asked.

"She was forced off the elevator on the eighth floor."

"Set up," Bolan snapped.

Sparks's hand went to the headphone on his right ear as he listened. "She just told them she didn't want to go into room 8014."

"It's over," Bolan said. "We're going now. We don't have time to take out the hit squad beforehand. Call my contact the organizer—have him get his student protesters into the street. Call the Red Sox fan and tell him we go now. I want all military posts around this resort under fire five minutes ago."

Sparks nodded. "Understood."

"Crash the hotel security system. Get Jack on the boat and in the river—I'm jerking Lerekhov out. I want you to burn this gear in place and get the hell out. Once I'm through this door, lock it and block it. You hear a knock, I want you out the window on the climbing rope. Get to Grimaldi, get into the river. Once I get Jill out I'm sending her after you, so keep our cell walkie-talkie modes up."

"Understood." Sparks paused. "This wasn't the way we planned it to go down."

Bolan nodded, understanding the agent's dismay. "It seldom does. Now let's roll."

A HARD MASCULINE HAND grabbed Jill Benson's breast and squeezed it cruelly through her blouse as she was manhandled into the room. Two hard-faced men in plainclothes stood sentry in front of the door as she was issued through.

She was thrown into a chair and her head yanked back by the hair when she tried to rise. She looked toward the man who was holding her and saw a pistol inches from her face. Instinctively she froze and felt handcuffs slide around her wrists, locking her hands into place behind her back.

She was stung by a slap that snapped her head around, and she felt blood in her mouth. Again the cruel fingers twisted into her hair and wrenched her head back.

This time she found herself looking into black, laughing eyes, and she felt fear.

"Did you think you could kill a man in our country and get away with it?"

"I killed no one," Benson stated in a clear, calm tone.

She had to stall, had to command their attention until Cooper arrived. She would tell them any lie just to eat up time. She looked away and spit blood out of her mouth onto the carpet.

The officer laughed. "I am a magic man. I know things." He leaned in close and leered. "It's my job to know things. People tell me things." He paused. "Now you'll tell me things, too."

Benson struggled to maintain a neutral look on her face. She could still feel the sting of the slap and knew her lips were puffing up.

"What do you want to know?" she asked.

She had no way of knowing who these men really were or who they thought she was. They wore uniforms but that meant nothing. She was in a suite at a resort hotel crawling with foreign intelligence operators. Their behavior and manner had been thuggish rather than coolly professional.

The backhand blow struck her across the cheek and snapped her head to the side. For the second time she tasted her own blood.

"I'll ask the questions," the man snarled.

He pulled a stainless-steel lighter from a pocket and began to absently play with it as he regarded her. His lips were full, almost feminine but with a quality that made Benson think of slugs.

He snapped the lighter open. Sparked a flame. Snapped the lighter closed. His eyes, the color of mud, watched her with predatory interest as he repeated the sequence. Behind him his men stood in a loose, silent phalanx. Guns were visible now. One man, the tallest of them, leered at her.

The main interrogator said something over his shoulder in a machine-gun dialect, sharp and dissonant to her ears. The others in the room chuckled in response. It was not a pleasant sound.

"Well, since you refuse to cooperate I'm afraid we'll have to take things up a notch." The man's voice was laconic. He snapped the lighter again.

"What!" Benson nearly screamed. "You haven't asked me anything yet!" Despite herself she was nearly frantic as she began to consider the implications of that flickering lighter flame.

"Oh?" The man feigned surprise. "You want to answer questions?"

"Sure." She nodded. Just killing time. Give him time, she told herself.

"How many men have you slept with?"

"What?" Her voice was a squawk even to her own ears.

"How many? In what ways? Were they big men, did you love it?"

"What!"

The interrogator was on her in a flash. He straddled her legs and pushed his weight down onto her lap, pinning her to the seat. He snatched her face up by the chin and jammed the muzzle of his pistol into her temple.

"I don't care what you know, whore, and I don't need you to tell me things."

He leaned in very close, his lips bare centimeters from Benson's own bruised and swollen mouth. His breath was hot against her skin, and she could feel his excitement against her stomach. She wanted to throw up.

"No," he continued. "I don't need you to learn things from. I need you to send a message."

His tongue flickered out and he licked a trail of blood from the corner of her mouth.

"To get my message across," he whispered, his eyes now bright, "I'm going to do things to you. My men are going to do things to you. Then we'll dump you and when they find you they'll know never—"

There was an angry shout in the hall then an unmistakable thud of something heavy falling against the door. The man was rising off her lap, twisting with the pistol when Benson lunged.

Her mouth found the side of his head and her teeth found the lobe of his ear. Her jaw snapped shut like a trap. The interrogator screamed in surprise even as his men were turning toward the door.

Bullets burned through the door, shattering the lock mechanism. A moment later the door snapped open, splintering along its length in the process with a sound like a gunshot. A sentry in plainclothes standing next to the door swiveled and swept a lethal-looking submachine gun out from under his suit jacket.

A dark and mangled shape came hurtling into the room. Gunfire erupted. She had a brief image of Cooper charging forward, a dead man in his arms as a shield like a tackling dummy. The corpse's head looked odd, like a deflated balloon. She could see the blue-gray scrambled-egg pieces of the dead man's brain sticking to his hair.

Benson jerked her head hard to the side and ripped the man's ear off. He screamed out loud and threw himself backward. Blood splashed her face as his weight lifted off her.

He rose and punched the bound woman hard in the face, knocking her over backward in the chair. She bounced off the hotel bed behind her and fell to the floor. She grunted with the impact and twisted to look up.

The interrogator loomed above her, blood soaking the side of his face and uniform. The pistol was in his hands. He lifted it and sighted down the barrel at her. His fat lips were pulled back over his teeth, and his muddy eyes were wild.

The shot sounded loud from so close, but it also merged

with the fierce gunfire echoing in the room. There was a muzzle-flash half a second after the man jerked to the side.

A 9 mm round burned into the bed next to Benson's head, tossing tick stuffing into the air. The interrogator spun and dropped forward, his gun falling from his slack hands. An exit wound had blown out his left eye and temple, turning it into a saucer-sized cavity.

The man's weight tumbled forward and flopped across the redheaded agent, crushing her bound hands cruelly against the thin carpet of the floor. The chair she had been secured to snapped under the pressure along its back and legs.

Benson grunted as the wind was driven from her under the impact. She struggled to rise. The bed blocked her view. Her own ragged breathing confused the sounds. She heard sharp curses and anguished cries and live bodies striking inanimate objects. From all around her the sharp, pungent scent of cordite sliced into her nose, burning it.

She struggled to lift the body off her by pushing up, but with her hands still bound behind her back it was nearly impossible. She scissor-kicked her legs and fought to rise. More of the man's blood spilled across her.

She got her head up and saw an Asian in plainclothes stumble backward, arms flung out wide, red geysers blossoming in his white dress shirt. She fought to rise, pulling her legs underneath her and shoving at the body. Her head cleared the edge of the bed and she saw bodies splayed across the room like abandoned toys. The walls were splashed with blood. The television screen had been shattered. A picture on the wall held the evidence of dual bullet impacts. A corpse, glassy-eyed and gory, lay sprawled belly down on the bed.

She twisted her head and saw Cooper locked in a deadly dance with the final survivor of the room's squad. She recognized the tallest man from the elevator. His uniform had been ripped open. He fought with Cooper over possession of the big American's pistol. She didn't quite comprehend what she was seeing, but suddenly Cooper bent at the waist, dropping his center of gravity, then rose again while twisting at the hips. He held the other man hard by the wrists and when he uncoiled his body the man tumbled over his own arms and was planted headfirst into the carpet.

Still holding on to the man's captured wrists, Cooper pointed the barrel of his weapon down and it fired three times in rapid succession. Benson could hear the wet, flat impacts of the rounds as they burrowed into flesh from brutally close range.

Cooper lifted his head and met hers eyes as she rose.

The moment ended in a heartbeat, and Cooper crossed the room and quickly worked to unlock her cuffs with the key he took from the dead interrogator's pocket.

"Thank you—" Benson began.

She wasn't gushing, just grateful and controlled though her heart was beating in her chest. She could still remember the feel of the men's hands on her body, insulting her sense of self, her dignity.

Cooper cut her off. "We've got to get moving. The plan is now maxed out. This changes everything. Here's one of the key-card controls Mitchell forged to operate the elevators."

Benson threw the cuffs down and quickly buttoned her shirt as she listened to Cooper's instructions. As he talked he reached down and took a pistol from a still warm corpse, jacked the slide and slid the weapon home behind her back.

"Go to the far end of the hall where the laundry service elevators are. Use that. Get to the ground and get the car 'cause Mitchell is going to be right behind you. I'm going directly for Lerekhov now, screw the hit team. I'll take it as it comes."

"What about your distractions? The professor and the Red Sox fan?"

"They've been mobilized. I don't know if they're fluid enough to get rolling in time, but the protest marches should provide enough cover for you two to get to the river should you end up on foot. Jack should be rolling and ready for extraction."

"I'm ready," Benson said, her voice firm.

Cooper smiled, half to himself, at her courage. She was a lioness.

"Good," he said.

He turned to go and Benson followed close behind him. He crossed the room, stepping around spreading pools of red. The enclosed space still reeked of cordite but a sweeter, more biological smell had already started to creep in. A fan turned overhead. Benson heard the hum of the air conditioner.

Cooper reached the door, his hands gripping his pistol. He quickly looked around the corner then ducked his head back. He stuck his head out again and took a fuller look. He turned toward the redhead.

"It's clear. You get to the service elevators. If there's a problem, shoot anyone armed. You've got to get out. I'm going to the stairs."

The two Americans stepped out into the hallway. Benson saw the crumpled heaps of the sentries she had seen on her way into the hotel room. Both men lay like discarded dolls with slack mouths and glassy eyes. Their spilling blood was very bright against the subdued hues of the hall carpet.

Benson reached out and grabbed his arm as he shrugged himself free of the knapsack. "Cooper, thank you. You take care of yourself."

"I will. You'll be fine—you have what it takes."

Then they ran.

19

Once Caine had the money the rest was mundane. There was nothing exotic about his purchases, and that, of course, was the beauty of it all. He didn't need covert connections or extralegal networks once he had the operating capital.

He went to the lawn-and-garden department of a home-improvement store, where he bought the fertilizer with the ammonium nitrate in an amount he thought wouldn't raise suspicion. He was putting in new lawn, a full acre of Kentucky Blue Grass. Then he drove across town and bought some more. Then he drove across town again and bought some more. Then he waited for the shift to change and he did it all again.

While he was at the store he wandered through the home-improvement aisles and picked up the washers, faucets screens, loose nuts and screws, the blowtorch, the power tools. It was all right there. He went to a toy store for the chemistry set. He bought two "because my nephews are almost the same age and I don't want them to fight."

At the hobby store he purchased the model rocket fuel. He purchased KNO3 from the pharmacy next door where the print on the bottles instructed him to use one-quarter teaspoon dissolved in water to promote diuretic action. To ensure he had enough of the potassium nitrate he bought several tubes of toothpaste, as well.

For powdered aluminum Caine simply hit the Internet. He found a multitude of sites willing to ship. He purchased the quantities he needed in discreet amounts from more than twenty sites, expedited shipping each time. For his primary source of hydrazine he repeated the dispersed-ordering process, this time buying industrial dyes.

The bombs were simple, so simple the risk of destroying himself was considerable but that came down to fear, and overcoming fear came down to wanting it bad enough. He stacked sealable plastic bins with fertilizer for the ammonium nitrate. Over the dry, loose bulk he added hydrazine at a ratio of two to one. The refining process from the dye to remove the hydrazine was not even necessary.

Using a pocket calculator he factored the amount of hydrazine in the dye per measured volume with the amount of ammonium nitrate per volume of fertilizer. All the numerical components for the problem were spelled right out on the package as per federal regulations. Despite the need for numerical calculations, he did not fall into the trap of digit summoning.

He now had a homebrew of the commercial substance Astrolite G. It was a compound slightly more powerful than the commercially manufactured TNT, offering him an impressive detonation velocity. Over this Caine mixed in the powdered aluminum and once it set, much like a birthday cake, he had made Astrolite A, a stable explosive causing a marked increase in density and brisance.

Shifting through foreign media reports, he was able to determine the amount in kilograms used by Iraqi terrorists to destroy the twenty-six-ton Bradley Infantry Fighting Vehicle. He put that much in the sedan. He doubled the amount he put in the tour van.

Now he needed to create triggers. Again it was laughably simply.

He purchased four prepaid cell phones. He knew he was leaving a record, a paper trail. There were simple steps he could have taken to obscure the trail, but it was always wise to give the devil his due.

There existed no single entity on the planet more capable of deciphering a paper trail than the U.S. Government. Maybe the French, but they had invented the word *bureaucracy* and it didn't really matter; once he acted the Feds would find his trail. He would most likely be dead, but it wasn't as if it was speed that would save him and nothing else.

In this case the trigger was simply a smaller detonation used to incite a larger explosion. For ease he went with picric acid, using a process taught by the CIA for their improvised-explosives course. It produced an explosive from aspirin.

Caine crushed a handful of aspirin tablets and then added water to make a chalky paste. He stirred ethyl alcohol into the aspirin paste and then filtered the solution to remove solid particles.

He painted the inside of the metal tube he would use as a container with epoxy while he waited for the ethyl alcohol in the aspirin to evaporate. Once that was done Caine recovered the remaining crystals.

He finished by pouring concentrated sulfuric acid from the children's chemistry sets into a large jar and added the crystals from the alcohol-aspirin solution. Feeling like a witch out of *Macbeth,* he heated the acid in simmering hot water bath for just over fifteen minutes. The acid turned a reddish color and he knew it had worked.

Next he added leftover potassium nitrate to the crystallized acid while stirring slowly. He let the acid cool to room temperature, then poured the amalgamation slowly into some water and let it cool down again. He filtered off the particles of picric acid and washed them with a cup of ice water.

He dried the crystals before packing them carefully into the epoxy-lined tube. He placed the tube onto a piece of wax paper before folding a length of wire into a hairpin loop and securing the loop in the tube, up against the wax paper. He added a few drops of epoxy in the tube and let it harden.

He cracked another beer and slowly chewed a Ritalin tablet while he waited for the epoxy to finish drying. He clicked his MP3 player up to his digital copy of AC/DC's "Back in Black" and let it play. The warning chimes and building riff of "Hell's Bells" filled his ears and he felt like the song was just his, for him, about him. The lyrics made promises he intended to fulfill. The bitter salt taste of the Ritalin was astringent in his mouth as he absorbed the drug through his inner cheek like a pinch of chewing tobacco.

Once the initial epoxy had set, Caine filled the rest of the tube with the picric acid. He carefully peeled the wax paper away from the tube and pushed the epoxy plug out of the tube. Taking a file Caine shaved the end of the plug, reducing the wire diameter at the loop.

Feeling like a medieval alchemist, Caine ground up a small amount of black powder from the caps designed for children's cap pistols with dextrin and water to make a paste that he coated along the wire loop. With sufficient voltage connected to the wire leads, the black powder would flash.

He then used a jeweler's screwdriver from an eyeglass-repair kit to open one of the prepaid cell phones. He attached the ringer activation wire directly to the wire loop. When he dialed the right number he would have his voltage. When he had his voltage he would have his flash. With the flash would come the trigger detonation. Following the initial detonation would be an explosion just like the one that had rocked Oklahoma City.

It was, literally, that easy.

20

Bolan moved down the hall at a brisk walk, his knapsack hanging casually off one shoulder. He looked hurried but not frantic; he didn't run. His weapon remained down and hidden. He wasn't in the business of killing security guards and local police. If he could avoid conflict, he would continue to do so.

But if actual players got in his way, whether military or foreign intelligence, he intended to go down fighting. He had committed himself, made a promise to the President that he would succeed and he was a man of his word.

He left the hall and hit the stairs, leaving Jill Benson behind him at the door to the service elevators after checking to make sure the area was empty. Once he hit the stairs he began to run up.

Lerekhov's delegation had clout commensurate with Vietnam's status at the conference and the code breaker had been given a deluxe suite some eight stories up from the room where the unknown players had taken Benson for "questioning."

The situation involving the dead body and the actors involved was already proving too murky for easy categorization, and Bolan realized he wouldn't have the time to arrive at satisfactory answers before events overtook him.

Whoever those players acted for, whatever their plans, Bolan had his own and he was hell-bent on sticking to them. He ran the stairs two at a time, his head up, eyes tracking for targets and suspicious movements. Like a grunt humping a heavy rucksack through the bush Bolan gutted it out.

Bolan's earpiece came to life and Sparks's voice broke through to give him an update.

"I have confirmation from Professor. His machine is running smoothly, and he had numbers in place already. Red Sox fan is loading his troops into position. We're cutting this so last minute I have doubts about him. I have just attempted landline contact with the room you're headed to now. Negative contact. Negative contact."

"Understood. Get what you can, scramble, meet our friend and scoot," Bolan replied.

"Understood." Sparks paused. "Good luck."

"Out."

Bolan jogged up the last flight of stairs and yanked open the fire door to the floor that Sparks's intelligence had identified being Lerekhov's. He stepped out of the heat of the stairwell and into the cool expanse of the hallway.

He began walking quickly down the corridor, his feet silent on the carpet. He shrugged off his knapsack and began to rummage in it as he approached his target door. He stopped in front of the dark-grained wooden door and double-checked the room number. Satisfied, he produced the key card Sparks had fabricated for him.

He pushed the key card into the slot above the door handle until the edge clicked against the bottom of the electric lock housing. He paused for a second, the lock indicator light showing red, then pulled his key card free. There was a pause. Then the red light winked out and a green light blinked on. He heard the dead bolt slide back automatically.

He turned the door handle and pushed. It moved easily

under the weight of his hand. As the door swung open, Bolan held his pistol in his free hand behind his back.

The Beretta was smooth and well balanced in his grip. The extra weight of the sound suppressor was negligible. His finger found the smooth curve of the trigger and took up the slack. Bolan pushed open the door.

He followed tight in behind the swing of the door, letting the knapsack drop to the ground just inside the doorway. He took up the Beretta pistol in both his hands and began tracking the muzzle in shorts snaps, dividing the room into instantaneous vectors then clearing them.

Mitchell Sparks's phone call to the hotel room had been only minutes earlier, indicating that the room was currently unoccupied though a search of hotel registry records by the cyber-specialist had revealed that a financial networks manager with the Philippine government and his wife were staying in the room.

Bolan had no intention of killing such innocent people, even in the name of operational security. He would get the jump on them, secure them, then execute his plan. The entire affair was rushed and last minute, but he had been dealt a distasteful hand of cards. He could give up, or he could push forward.

He stepped into the room. The lights were off, the television dark. He could hear no sounds coming from the bathroom but he checked it anyway, then the closets. He had caught a break at least in that the room appeared completely unoccupied.

He moved to the door, threw the latch, secured the dead bolt, then rammed a desk chair up under the handle. He picked up his knapsack and went to the left-hand wall between the beds.

He reached down and ripped the phone out of the wall, then tossed it onto the other bed, followed by the lamp and a digital clock. He slid the Beretta into his waistband behind his back and then stooped. His hands found either corner of the nightstand and picked it up. Casually he tossed it over the bed, where it landed on the carpeted floor with a muted clatter.

He opened his knapsack and took out a compact apparatus that resembled a caulking gun used by industrial plumbers. With quick, efficient movements he attached the tube containing the foam explosive and then added the second, smaller tube of propellant.

He stepped forward and began spreading a slurry of foam explosive on the wall. It splattered across the wallpaper like shaving cream. The compound splashed onto the wall in thick, muddy streams, and Bolan hastily drew a zigzag pattern starting about seven feet above the floor and moving down.

The applicator made a sputtering sound as it emptied its bladder, and Bolan casually dropped it on the floor at his feet. It bounced once and came to rest against the wall. Bolan pulled a timing pencil from a slit on his knapsack and pushed it into the viscous goo after initiating the detonator.

Moving quickly, Bolan backpedaled from between the beds and moved to put the retaining wall next to the entrance between himself and coming blast. A tracer round could have been used to detonate the foam, as well, but he preferred the more controlled method of a timing pencil.

He went to one knee beside the wall and drew the Beretta once again.

He inhaled, then slowly exhaled. He kept his mouth slack to allow for compensation for the concussive pressure in his ears. The muscles along his frame were primed but loose, like a jungle predator before the killing leap. He shrugged the knapsack into place. Now was the time.

The explosion was sharp and sudden. It clapped loud like a thunderhead and a cloud of plaster dust and construction material billowed into the room. Bolan was up, coming to his feet smoothly and snapping the machine pistol in his fists out ahead of him.

He rounded the corner and plunged between the beds, slipping into the smoke like a violent apparition. He moved forward in a half crouch and breached the hole he'd just blown through the wall. He stepped over a small lip of structural support left intact on the ground.

Emerging into the adjoining hotel room, he scanned for the Vietnamese security forces. He saw a man at his feet struggling to rise, a Makarov pistol half-pulled from a shoulder sling.

Bolan lowered the muzzle of the Beretta and it coughed a 3-round burst, the pistol recoiling smoothly in his grip, the barrel barely rising off target. Enough blood and brain to fill a soup bowl was splashed out on the carpet behind the man's head, and Bolan stepped across his corpse.

The Executioner caught a flash of movement out of the corner of his eye and saw a snarling Vietnamese in a cheap business suit sprawled out on a bed. The man swept up a sub-machine gun, swinging the muzzle around toward the intruder.

Bolan directed twin bursts into his throat and chest, staining his pillow crimson and knocking the security agent back. Instantly Bolan pivoted back around at the waist even as he advanced a few more steps into the room.

He saw a figure push itself up off the floor between the beds. His eyes narrowed, and his finger tensed on the trigger. He identified the man as European and held his fire. Beyond the bed next to the rising Occidental, another figure, this one in a crisp gray-and-maroon uniform, leaped forward.

There was a starburst of flame as the pistol in the uni-formed man's hand came to life even as Bolan was throwing himself to the side. Bolan squeezed the Beretta's trigger as he leaped but the rounds went wide and punched holes out through the window behind the enemy gunmen.

He heard the pistol's angry bark as he landed on the bed next to the corpse of the second man he'd killed. Bouncing up, Bolan twisted his torso into position as two 9 mm rounds of enemy fire slapped into the wall of the hotel room.

Bolan's shot was hasty and he scored only a gut wound. The Vietnamese bodyguard staggered, one hand flying to his leaking belly. Bolan shot again and put a triburst in the man's shoulder, chest and throat.

Blood sprayed out and seemed to hang in the air for a moment as the man sagged. The soldier dropped to the floor and his own blood rained down on him. Bolan twisted to cover the front of the room in case there was another member of the security entourage in the room.

Seeing nothing, he turned back and rose from the bed. The European had managed to struggle to his feet, obviously still discombobulated from the initial blast. From less than two feet away Bolan took in his features and recognized his target. Without hesitation Bolan surged forward and snatched the man by the collar of his shirt.

The Russian squawked in surprise then, and Bolan bowled him over, driving him onto the bed and flat on his back. The Executioner was on him like a wolf on a lamb. The muzzle of the Beretta was shoved up under the man's chin in the soft bar of his jaw. The man's eyes grew wide in terror.

Bolan leaned in close.

"You are one wrong answer away from death, Comrade," he said. "I want to know what a Communist true believer so ardent he left Russia for Vietnam after *glasnost* is doing with a sudden change of heart this late in the game."

The man swallowed and Bolan saw his Adam's apple bob

with the effort. Lerekhov was so frightened the sound came out in a dry click. The man answered in English.

"Didn't your handlers explain everything to you?" His voice was weak but frantic.

"Wrong answer, Comrade," Bolan snarled back. "You see my handlers? You see anyone else? The clock is ticking, so you convince me!"

"Fine!" The old man coughed. "I'm dying! Can't you see it? Can't you smell it?" He shook with indignation. "Cancer of the blood."

Bolan's eyes narrowed as they hunted for confirmation. The phlegm rattle in Lerekhov's voice supported his claim. Bolan saw the yellowed sclera of his eyes, the gaunt features. He could smell the fetid breath that whistled and echoed as the man gasped his claim. It fit the story he'd been given, and this close up Bolan was inclined to believe him.

"What's the matter? The worker's paradise not have good enough health care?"

"Damn you!" the man snapped angrily. He became so emotional he slipped back into Russian, apparently without noticing. "It is for my mother! For my mother. I broke her heart. She was Russian Orthodox. It broke her heart when I joined the Party. I buried her in a state grave, not in a church. I am dying. No medicine could touch my pain. It was in my guts, in my bones the agony. Finally I—I broke. I broke and I prayed. I prayed for the first time since I was a little boy."

Lerekhov stopped, his tongue went to his lips and Bolan eased back on the pressure of his muzzle under the old man's chin. He had only seconds to make a decision about whether or not he believed the veteran code breaker. Bolan was used to making those kinds of decisions.

"I prayed," Lerekhov said, "and the pain eased. I knew then,

I understood then how wrong I had been, how I had hurt her. I want only to be buried by a priest of the orthodoxy when I die. I want only for my mother's body to be moved now to hallowed ground. If you will promise me that, I will tell your government whatever you want. That is all. Laugh if you want. Scoff if you want. I do not care but if you do not believe the truth because it is so simple, then kill me now. Hurry, damn you!"

Bolan stood. He began shrugging off his backpack. "Get up," he told the man. "I'm getting you out of here."

"Thank God," the old man muttered, speaking English again.

Outside the window shattered by Bolan's bullets he heard the first of a dozen explosions as the Myanmar guerrillas began to spring their ambush. As Lerekhov rose, Bolan pulled a hard plastic case about six inches square from out of the knapsack.

"What's that?" The old man asked, suspicious as Bolan flipped open the latches.

Bolan looked up and captured the man's gaze with his own. "You're going to have to trust me. You're not going to want to, but we don't have time. I'm going to give you a shot. If you refuse the shot, I leave you. I want those Iranian codes, but you have to play my way."

As he spoke, Bolan pulled out a syringe filled with a yellowish liquid. The old man's eyes grew wide when he saw it, but the Russian set his mouth into a firm line and grimly began rolling up the sleeve of his shirt.

"Never mind that." Bolan shook his head. "I don't need a vein. This shot is intramuscular. Just put your leg out."

"Can I ask what it is?" Lerekhov said.

Bolan could hear how the man's pride was keeping his apprehension in check and felt a grudging admiration start to grow.

"It's a go-shot. We've got a very tough ten minutes ahead of us, Andrei. I've manipulated the board as best I can, but there are just too damn many pieces in play. I need you to move, but you're not in the best shape for that with your illness. This is your best and only chance of making it."

"My heart—" the Russian code breaker began.

"I know," Bolan cut him off. "We made allowances. I don't have time. *You* don't have time. What's it going to be?"

Bolan kept the bite out of his voice. He had turned a corner in his own mind about the old man.

Lerekhov drew his mouth tight and then nodded. He sat on the edge of the bed and stuck out his leg. Bolan reached out and grabbed the man's leg by the quadriceps through the loose weave of his trousers. It was like grabbing a stick it was so skinny, but he was able to pinch enough flesh to do the job.

Without preamble he slid the needle through the pants and directly into the defector's leg muscle, such as it was. He quickly flexed his finger and dumped the injection into the Russian. Lerekhov winced as the medicine pushed in between the fibers of his muscle.

Once the plunger had been pushed down to the bottom of the barrel, Bolan pulled the needle free and stuck it unceremoniously into the mattress. He looked at Lerekhov, searching for the signs of a characteristic response.

The man's rheumy brown eyes dilated even as he watched until the black of the iris had almost obliterated any trace of the brown cornea. A heartbeat later a thick sheen of sweat appeared on the Russian's forehead and upper lip, his face became pale and his nostrils flared as he began to breath faster.

"My God!" the code breaker exclaimed. "I feel like I'm going to explode."

"Good, it's time to roll. I won't leave you but try to stay close. If something happens get down and keep me between you and the bad guys."

Bolan shrugged into his knapsack even as heavy machine-gun fire began to answer the rocket attacks outside. Hell had come to Yangon. Bolan had paid good money for the distraction, and his instructions had been clear; the only targets the guerrilla group would engage were established military checkpoints. The attack was to last no longer than twelve minutes, and they should avoid any action that might lead to collateral damage.

Bolan rose and turned toward the door to the room. Barely three minutes had elapsed since he had detonated the foam and breached the wall. Behind him Lerekhov came off the bed like a jack-in-the-box.

Bolan's finger went to his earpiece.

"How we doing?"

"It's going on out here!" Sparks shouted back, his voice jubilant. "It's chaos. The lady got out and got the car. All my memory cards have been wiped. The contact to guide us through the mob is in the car. We are headed toward the river now. The Red Sox fans caught the soldiers sleeping!"

"Copy. I'm in phase two," Bolan acknowledged. He began moving toward the door. "Let's roll," he told the Russian, but the older man was already close on his heels.

21

Bolan stepped into the hallway.

The corridor was jammed with milling, frightened people. Behind him Lerekhov hovered as if tethered to his wrist. Bolan used his height to scan above the throng. Scared people were wincing at every explosion that echoed into the hotel from outside, shuddering at the noise of machine guns returning fire.

Bolan frowned. For every scared diplomat or bureaucrat there were two hard-eyed men with hands tucked into the lapels of their jackets. Bolan stepped to the side and let the ex-Soviet code breaker move forward according to his instructions.

Lerekhov began to navigate the hall, heading toward the far end away from the guest elevators, fighting the flow of guests. After a moment Bolan followed him. People bumped into the old man and pushed past him in their hurry to reach the elevator lobby but mostly ignored him. The man was so juiced up from his shot he actually seemed to gather forward propulsion from the kinetic energy of each contact and brush by.

Halfway down the hallway, barely fifteen seconds out of the room, Bolan faced his first obstacle. A fat Asian man followed by a tiny stick of a woman in too much makeup burst out of a door directly by Bolan. The big American turned a shoulder into them and they split around him, arguing loudly in a language he didn't immediately recognize.

At the same time from just over his shoulder he heard an

angry Vietnamese voice shout Lerekhov's name. Just as Bolan had instructed, the Russian put his chin into his chest, ignored the voice and pushed forward.

The man barked another angry command, and Bolan stepped into the slight well offered by the open door to the room from which the fat Asian and his companion had emerged. A member of the Vietnamese auxiliary security team, dressed in his parade uniform of gray and crimson, shoved his way past Bolan's position, eyeing the big American, then turning his attention back toward his charge.

As he stepped past the American, Bolan saw the man clutched a Makarov pistol behind his back. Bolan stepped back into the hallway, coming up directly behind the Vietnamese soldier.

The medulla oblongata, Bolan knew, was Latin for "stem of the rose." It was specifically that part of the brain stem that joined the brain and the skull to the spine. It was the arterial nexus of the central nervous system.

Bolan lifted up a big right hand and fired knuckles the size of dice into the back of the man's neck at the medulla oblongata. The effect was as instantaneous and as final as the industrial trip-hammer at a slaughterhouse. The Vietnamese buckled at the knees and dropped to the carpet.

The Makarov tumbled loose from slack fingers and bounced off the carpet. Bolan slid the fallen pistol into the open door of the room. He bent over and lifted the 145-pound man like a sack of potatoes and tossed the limp body into the open room. He leaned forward, snagged the door handle and pulled the door closed.

He pushed his way into the crowd. Three seconds had elapsed.

Up ahead the fleeing Lerekhov had almost reached the end of the hall. He looked back once and Bolan angrily gestured for him to keep moving, but a look of horror splashed across the Russian's animated face. The Executioner knew without looking that things had not gone smoothly.

He rudely pushed his way forward through the crowd like a running back fighting his way upfield. He tossed a look over his shoulder and saw more uniformed Vietnamese standing at the door to Lerekhov's room.

The men held Shipka Bulgarian submachine guns. The Shipka was a boxy, straightforward design, using simple blowback operation and firing from open bolt. The lower receiver along with pistol grip and trigger guard, were made from polymer, while the upper receiver was made from steel. The simple buttstock was made from steel wire and folded to the left side of gun.

It was an easily concealed compact weapon perfectly designed for urban operations and was capable of firing 700 rounds per minute. Exactly the situation Bolan wanted to avoid in such a congested environment.

He did the only thing he could do.

He ran.

JUST AHEAD OF HIM Lerekhov pushed open the door at the end of the hall that opened onto the staircase. The Russian disappeared through the doorway. Bolan cursed in frustration; at the end of the hall, set in a sort of L-shape were *two* doors. One was the fire door that led to the hotel stairs, and the other opened up to the service elevators used by the resort's maids and other employees.

Lerekhov had become confused and had taken the wrong door.

Toward the end of the hall the congestion of milling people suddenly, dramatically cleared and Bolan could move in an unrestricted fashion. He lengthened his stride, ignoring the angry shouts in Vietnamese coming from behind him. He didn't display his weapon or attempt to give them any overt reason to open fire.

Despite his restraint a line of slugs chewed into the wall just over Bolan's shoulder and the acoustic chamber of the hallway carried the gunfire reports painfully to his ears like claps of thunder.

He raced forward and hit the fire door with his shoulder, knocking it open. Looking up, he saw Lerekhov running up the staircase in front of him. He lunged forward, throwing the door closed behind him to slow pursuit.

"Get out at the next floor, get out at the next floor!" Bolan shouted in Russian.

Lerekhov didn't acknowledge him in his chemically augmented frenzy. Bolan couldn't be sure the man had actually even heard him. As he put on a fresh burst of speed to overtake the older man, Bolan marveled at the potency of the shot he'd given the Russian. The sickly seventy-something was moving like a man thirty years younger.

Bolan finally caught up with the scrambling Lerekhov. He jerked the running man to a stop by his shirt and leaned in close.

"Didn't you hear me calling you?" he demanded.

"You told me not to stop when I heard people yelling at me!" Lerekhov protested.

Bolan cursed. "You're supposed to be a genius? Go through this door onto the floor, get into the service elevator room like I told you!"

Lerekhov bobbed his head enthusiastically and reached for the handle of the fire door. Bolan saw the handle turning at the last moment and realized someone was coming through from the other side.

Bolan leaped forward, knocking the code breaker to the side, and jerked the door open, seizing the initiative. The door opened and Bolan found himself face-to-face with a Myanmar security guard in the ridiculously formal uniform of hotel security. The man had a pistol in a holster on his web belt and a long black nightstick was clutched in one fist. A second security guard shuffled forward behind the first man.

Bolan reached out with his right hand and grabbed hold of the nightstick. He crushed down hard on the baton, locking it into place. His left hand fired out in a brawler's roundhouse, clipping the Myanmar guard in the ear.

The man sagged against the doorjamb, dazed but still conscious. Bolan rotated his shoulder back and brought his next punch downstairs while the man attempted to cover his head from the second blow.

Bolan's punch drove into the man's side, bruising past his lower rib cage and muscle pack to pummel his liver. The man gasped in sudden, electric pain and crumpled to the floor. As the guy sagged, Bolan snapped up his knee and caught the falling man on the point of his chin, putting his lights out.

Bolan twirled the nightstick in smooth, tight revolution and brought it down like a hand ax into the unprotected neck of the second resort guard, dropping him, as well. The man fell in a stupor across the crumpled heap of his partner.

Bolan tossed the baton aside and reached out to grab the nearly hyperventilating Lerekhov and pushed him past the unconscious security guards.

"Move!" he snapped.

The ex-Soviet code breaker hopped over the splayed limbs of the unconscious guards, darting into the guest-room area of the resort. From below them on the staircase Bolan heard fire doors slam as someone charged through them into the stairwell.

He risked a look as Lerekhov went through the door. He saw the ugly angry faces of part of the code breaker's security detail, Shipkas in hand. One, perhaps an officer, looked up and the two men locked gazes. The Vietnamese screamed something in outrage and Bolan ducked back.

He knew he didn't have time to remove the trail of breadcrumbs left by the unconscious heaps of the security guards. He hopped over the downed men and pushed open the door, stepping out into a hotel hallway identical from the one he had just fled. He saw the door to the service area just off at a right angle and plunged through it.

He saw a long narrow room filled with extra room service trays, unattended vacuum cleaners and an old mop in a bucket.

He was pulling a skeleton fire key out of a small pocket on the knapsack even as Lerekhov anticipated his need and pushed the old freight elevator's up button. While they waited for the elevator car to arrive, Bolan pulled his Beretta free and covered the door.

He spared a glance for the heavily breathing code breaker. The man was sucking in great lungfuls of air and his face was no longer pale, but flushed. Still, his gaze was sharp and he seemed more focused now. His foot tapped and Bolan thought the old man might just make it through the last, long yards of the run.

The elevator arrived with an anachronistic ding and the scratched and dented doors slid apart. Bolan had his machine pistol up and ready as the doors slid open to reveal an empty car.

Lerekhov jumped inside and his finger, knuckles gnarled, pushed the last button to the uppermost floor reached by the elevator. Bolan slid in beside him and shoved the counterfeit fire service key into the access lock set into the control panel. He snapped the key counterclockwise and bypassed the default settings, taking control of the elevator.

The door to the service area burst open, and a frantic-faced Vietnamese ducked his head inside, panting and casting wildly about. He saw the elevators doors sliding closed and lunged forward, bringing up the Shipka.

There was a slight cough from the sound suppressor as Bolan put a 9 mm round into the man's throat at three yards before the doors shut. The elevator started up with a lurch. Bolan turned toward Lerekhov, who had pressed himself up against the wall.

"It's almost over," he told the man. "The team will leave someone to wait to see what floor the elevator stops on while they send others up the staircase. We don't have time to try to fool them—this is a race."

Lerekhov nodded once, indicating his understanding.

"When we come to a stop," Bolan continued, "I go through first. Stay close. We'll be one staircase below the roof door. Once we're through that we just need to make it across to the river side of the property, then we'll go down and head for the water."

"The riots, the guerrilla attacks on the police positions, that was—"

"Me, yes," Bolan acknowledged. "The more that's going on street-side the less people we'll have between us and my ride on the water. All you have to do is bust your ass getting across the roof. If you do that, I'll get you out of here."

"I feel like I could run all day!" Lerekhov said.

"That's only going to last a couple of more minutes," Bolan warned. "It's the most we could do and not put your heart in too great a peril. I have intelligence there is a hit team after you. Do you know anything about that?"

"Could be Chinese intelligence, could be the Cambodians." Lerekhov didn't seem surprised by the news. "I've done damage to both of those countries' espionage programs against Vietnam. It could be someone else, but I was briefed last month that about those two."

"In the end I suppose it doesn't matter—just look alive when we move."

The service elevator jerked to a halt and the doors slid open. Bolan shuffled through, his weapon up, and cleared the area before Lerekhov followed him. Immediately Bolan crossed the service area to the door.

"Come on, they know where we are now. They'll be coming," he said.

"Go, lead. I follow," Lerekhov huffed.

Bolan jerked open the door and saw a startled maid in a burgundy dress with a gold name tag. She was plump, pretty and in her forties. She squealed in terror and hurried away down the hall. Bolan ignored her.

The Executioner raced through the door leading to the staircase, the code breaker close behind him. He looked downward and saw nothing, but the sound of feet hammering on the metal staircase was undeniable. He saw a door, this marked with a metal plaque covered in red writing. He tried the door handle just to double-check and found it locked.

He looked over his shoulder back down the staircase—Lerekhov was hovering nearby—then reached into a side pouch of his knapsack and removed his lock-pick gun. He slid the prongs into the lock housing set into the door handle and squeezed the lever.

There was a mechanical jolt and a satisfying click as the mechanism rotated under the pressure, unlocking the door. He turned the knob and pulled the roof access door open, his finger going to his earpiece. He broke radio silence.

"We are making entry to the roof now."

Sparks, having obviously been waiting for this signal, answered immediately. "Copy. Transport is ready."

"Copy, out."

Bolan signaled Lerekhov and rushed him through the door. He heard footsteps coming up the stairwell on the floor below them and he slammed his door shut. He turned the lock set into handle, relocking the access door.

He heard Lerekhov pounding up the stairs and turned. A single-run stair led up to scaffolding. A final metal fire door was set at the end of the scaffolding.

Bolan followed the code breaker up the final steps to the door. The ex-Soviet waited for Bolan, and when he tried the handle the heavy door swung open easily enough. Just below them the roof access door rattled violently as bodies thumped into it. Gunfire rang out, and several bullets burst through the handle housing on the door.

"Let's go!" Bolan shouted.

The two men stumbled out onto the roof.

It was a strange industrial landscape filled with conduit housing, exposed pipes, maintenance shacks and HVAC units. The space was so cluttered that it formed a obstacle course, and running across the roof would be like a sprinter racing hurtles.

"Come on, we've got to make the other side," Bolan commanded. "Just run to the far edge."

He pushed the older man forward, letting him get a head start while he covered their rear. Lerekhov put two hands on a waist-high length of pipe, shiny with insulation and as thick as his leg. He cleared the obstacle, darted between two giant climate-control units and darted out of sight for a moment.

The door to the access stairs burst open. Bolan was waiting. He triggered his pistol and put two 3-round bursts into the structure. The metal scarred with divots under the 9 mm impacts and sparks flew. The door swung shut again.

Bolan turned and ran.

He twisted and leaped, darting over and around obstacles. He caught up to Lerekhov at the point where the roof they were on suddenly dropped two stories. The Russian was navigating an enclosed maintenance ladder.

Bolan dropped to one knee beside the lip of the roof and turned to face the way he had come, bringing up his pistol. Periodically he peeked over the edge to gauge Lerekhov's progress. He could hear the sound of rocket and machine-gun fire clearly now. Dark columns of smoke twisted up into the air from nearby.

A Vietnamese darted around an industrial blower housing the size of an automobile, Shipka up and ready in his hands.

Bolan fired. His burst caught the man in the stomach and folded him over. His second burst tore off the top of his head and cast brain matter across the roof. The downed soldier's comrades appeared behind them and opened fire with their Shipka submachine guns.

Bolan rolled across his shoulder as rounds tore up the asphalt roof around him. He slid over the edge of the roof and dropped his pistol, letting it fall. He caught the outside cage of the maintenance ladder and scrambled down, using only his hands.

He let go about twelve feet above the second, lower roof and dropped. He struck the roof and rolled. He gained his feet and lunged for the pistol he'd been forced to drop, shouting for the gasping Lerekhov to run. The deadly Italian pistol was unharmed by the fall.

Bolan scooped up the Beretta and began scrambling backward. He saw forms at the building edge, now commanding the high ground. He shot across the distance in a feat of exceptional marksmanship, and the man tumbled over the lip, falling to collapse in a motionless heap below.

The final two members of the squad rushed to the lip of the building and went to one knee, raising their submachine guns.

Bolan sprinted for cover.

22

Bolan darted around an obstruction, skipping over some electrical conduits set only a few inches above the roof as he did. The Vietnamese behind him opened fire and bullets sang off the roof around him, igniting sparks and spraying a hail of pebbles. He knew the range was extreme for accurate submachine gun or pistol fire, but the sheer volume of rounds allowed for the possibility of lucky shots.

He found Lerekhov bent over, his hands on his knees and gasping for breath. Bolan ran up and put a strong hand under the older man's arm. Lerekhov looked at him, and his eyes were starting to become glassy from the fatigue. The man let loose with a cough and something rattled low in his chest.

"We're almost there, Andrei," Bolan said. "We're almost there."

Lerekhov nodded once and began to rise. Bolan set off in a jog, still keeping his hand on the Russian's arm for stability and to increase the man's speed.

They ducked through the obstacle course on the roof, then came to an open area. Bolan led the run across the danger zone. On the far side of the danger area the hotel roof rose like the prow of a ship, and there was a maintenance ladder identical to the one they had scrambled down. This one led upward.

Lerekhov's breathing was ragged as they ran. He cried out

in pain and his hand flew to his side. Bolan realized the man had a runner's cramp, then just as quickly realized there was nothing to be done. He began to drag the Russian along behind him, bearing his weight, forcing each step out of him. The old man's cough now sounded wet, and Bolan was starting to breathe hard himself.

They reached the enclosed ladder and Bolan pushed Lerekhov forward.

"Go, climb," he ordered.

Dutifully the old man moved forward and began to climb. His movements were tortured and excruciatingly slow. Rung by rung he began to ascend the ladder. Bolan gritted his teeth in frustration and turned to cover the man's climb.

He realized that if he waited to hold off the remaining Vietnamese, he'd be caught on the ladder himself. There was no good option. Cursing, he turned and entered the safety cage of the ladder. He tucked his pistol into his shoulder holster and started to climb.

He scrambled up quickly behind Lerekhov, his hands going to the outside of the ladder. He put a shoulder under the man's butt and pushed upward, taking some of his weight and making it easier for him to move his arms and legs.

Something low in his back spasmed in protest at the awkward angle of the weight bearing, but Bolan gritted his teeth like a power lifter and he drove upward, shoving Lerekhov up the ladder.

The cacophony of explosions and gunfire from beyond the roof was suddenly punctuated by the sharper reports of weapons firing close by. Without looking, Bolan realized the Vietnamese had arrived.

Bullets chattered into the wall below him and rattled off

the metal safety cage. Bolan dug his foot onto the next rung, flexed the big muscles of his quadriceps, took up slack with his arms and heaved Lerekhov upward.

The slightly built older man shot upward, his own hands now fairly flying up the rungs. The Russian reached the top and tumbled over the edge of the building. Bullets walked up the wall in hot pursuit as Bolan came over the top and rolled to safety behind the roof's edge.

Automatically Bolan's hand found the butt of his pistol as he rolled over. He heard the sharp words of an Asian language he didn't recognize coming from scant yards away. The voice was authoritarian and angry, and Bolan triangulated the approximate position of the speaker while still not seeing the man.

Lerekhov bellowed a warning. Bolan finished his roll, flipping his legs toward the new threat as his pistol cleared holster leather.

He had the impression of a figure in dark clothing, saw the Kalashnikov in the man's hands and pulled his trigger. Two of his rounds struck the bolt housing on the assault rifle and the third made the distinctive slapping sound of a bullet striking Kevlar.

Bolan lifted the muzzle of the Beretta, following the recoil, and blew off the man's face from less than two yards away. He saw an Asian in black, SWAT-style fatigues tumble away, the AK-104 Kalashnikov carbine falling away. Something else struck the asphalt of the roof. A black box.

Bolan blinked, focused. He saw that the black box was a Chinese model of a Detonics laser range finder. The effective range on an AK-104 precluded the need for the range finder. The range finder was for distance shooting.

Spotter, Bolan realized.

The man was part of a sniper team deployed to the roof.

Bolan sat up, then hunched over as submachine-gun rounds from the Vietnamese poured over the lip of the building. Lerekhov screamed once and blood geysered from his shoulder as he was knocked to the ground.

As the Russian fell, Bolan saw behind him. Another Asian soldier in reflective sunglasses and black fatigues was scrambling off a shooter's pad beside the edge of the building facing the street. A Soviet SVD sniper rifle was in his hands, and the man was trying desperately to bring the unwieldy long gun to bear. Bolan had a heartbeat to act. To act or to die.

He shot the man, putting two rounds into his head. The man sagged, blood gushing from the exit wound in his skull. Bolan's slide locked open and he dropped his empty magazine, reaching to his shoulder holster to pull another free.

He slapped it home, dropped the catch on the bolt and chambered a round. Lerekhov moaned in agony as he lay on the roof. Blood was all over him, soaking his shirt.

Bolan slammed his Beretta back into its shoulder and snatched up the AK-104 from the first man in the sniper team he had killed. He quickly checked it, then rolled back across his stomach and came up against the lip of the building.

Without looking, he shoved the muzzle of the carbine over the edge and fired off a long burst of harassing fire. Keeping the trigger down, he did a crunch movement and sneaked a peek over the lip.

He saw the Vietnamese soldiers scrambling for cover after crossing two-thirds of the roof. Bolan showed them no mercy. He rose to one knee and used his superior firepower to finish the battle. The men spun and stumbled as the rounds slammed into them. They were driven flat on the roof, and Bolan raked them with his carbine.

Satisfied, he flung away the smoking weapon and turned

toward the code breaker. He raced forward and hauled the man to his feet. Lerekhov's legs buckled and he sagged in Bolan's grip.

Whatever boost the injection had given him was gone. Lerekhov looked up into Bolan's eyes, tried to smile, then his head sagged.

"No!" Bolan snarled.

Frantic, his fingers went to the man's neck, feeling for a pulse. Though weak, a pulse was present. The old man had merely succumbed to shock and fatigue. Bolan lifted him in his arms, stood and began to race the last fifty yards to safety.

At the far edge of the building Bolan couldn't rouse Lerekhov. His pulse was thready and weak but present and the man still breathed, but he would not wake up. Bolan cursed and laid him down.

Working quickly, he shimmied out of his knapsack and reached inside and drew out the rappel ribbon he had secured there along with a harness. He worked quickly, sliding on the rappel harness and a welder's glove while ignoring the sounds of gunfire and explosions coming from the city side of the resort.

He found a communications satellite relay to handle the hotel's international television and clipped the rappel ribbon around it, then ran it through the twin D-rings on his harness. He dropped the coil of ribbon over the edge and moved over to the immobile Lerekhov. The man's eyes fluttered, but he didn't rouse and Bolan was through trying.

He felt empathy for the old man, respected how much he'd risked to come this far. "I'll get you out," he promised. He bent and yanked the man up before ducking and draping him over his shoulder.

With good technique and a solid harness, rappelling could easily be conducted with only one hand. For military applications this allowed a weapon to be fired and certain specific methods such as the face-first Australian style had been adapted to capitalize on that.

For Bolan it meant he could keep one arm around the unconscious code breaker and control his descent from a single fist tucked behind his right hip. He stepped over to the edge of the building and looked down. He saw some civilians running across the lawns and gardens set between the hotel and the river. They didn't look up and he remained unnoticed.

He stepped over the edge, balanced briefly, then lowered himself smoothly until his legs were parallel to the ground. He kicked out away from the wall and bounded down, tightly controlling his speed by squeezing his fist around the sliding ribbon.

As always, physical prowess was a paycheck Bolan cashed time and again in his War Everlasting. Like a professional athlete he lived or died, excelled or failed, according to his state of fitness. Mental toughness and battle-tested instincts were indispensable, but they relied on a body in peak physical condition.

The Executioner dropped the fifteen stories in leapfrog movements, kicking away from the wall, falling, swinging in, kicking out again, dropping farther. The rope screamed as it slid through his grasp, and the heat was building up across his palm, threatening to create a friction burn.

Lerekhov was a still, inert weight over his shoulder. Bolan slid down the last two stories in a final jump and quickly unhooked the excess ribbon from the D-rings on his harness. He was pleased with his progress so far. He had managed to move a well-guarded target across nearly a dozen internal-security checkpoints from various forces and the ubiquitous eyes of the security cameras and put him down just yards from the extraction point.

With the code breaker still on his shoulder Bolan turned and began to run toward the sluggish brown water of the big river. He shook the welder's glove off his right hand, which still smarted from the friction of the rope, and drew his pistol.

The attack by his allies in the KNLA guerrilla group had been meant to distract the better coordinated and armed military and security units away from Bolan's route. Several blocks over from the ambush, police forces were tied up managing the riotous crowds.

All he had to do was make it to the river.

A knot of Asian civilians he had seen on his rappel down suddenly turned toward him. Bolan's veteran instincts began to scream. He saw a blocky Asian man with fish-paste skin suddenly throw a half-smoked cigarette to the ground and lift an expensive cell phone while slapping a slender companion to his right.

The skinny man whirled and his eyes widened when he saw Bolan race past them with the unconscious Lerekhov thrown unceremoniously over one shoulder. The man plunged his hand into a brown canvas suitcase and reemerged with a cut-down Chinese shotgun.

No, Bolan thought as he pivoted, not the hit team. He raised the Beretta as the man tossed the suitcase away, all pretenses gone. Just over the shotgun-wielding killer's shoulder Bolan saw two more Asian men in the same plain, dark suits running toward them.

Their briefcases and duffel bags were discarded as submachine guns appeared in their fists. He stroked the trigger on his Beretta, firing from the hip. The shotgunner sagged as a triburst hammered into his chest. Beside him the killer with the cell phone was clawing for a pistol under his jacket.

Bolan, still sprinting, shot him on the fly, striking him high on the shoulder in his haste. As he adjusted his aim, he realized he wasn't going to beat the men behind the initial pair to the trigger. He shot the cell phone hitter as he dived forward, letting Lerekhov hit the ground and sprawl across the grass.

The pair racing toward the battle lifted their weapons, and desperately Bolan tried to bring his own pistol around to bear. He hit the ground and rolled, flinging his gun hand out straight and trying to take aim.

The pair of gunners suddenly began to twist and jerk like marionettes in the hands of a crazed puppeteer. Jets of scarlet burst from them in arcs and craters were blown out of their shirts and flesh. An instant later Bolan heard the staccato hammering of an assault rifle.

He turned his head toward the river and saw Charlie Mott in the bow of a rigid-hull assault craft. The Stony Man freelance pilot lay belly down on the edge of the boat, an M-4 carbine chattering in his hands.

"Come on!" he yelled.

Bolan jumped to his feet as Mott scrambled backward toward the stem of the raft where the twin outboard engines purred with suppressed energy. Bolan reached down and jerked Lerekhov up by the collar, then stooped and bear-hugged the man.

He squeezed the old man to his chest and ran, the frantic beating of the code breaker's heart evident against the birdcage of his ribs. Bolan scrambled down the bank and into the water.

He grunted with the effort as he heaved the Russian into the boat. Bolan closed one hand across the gunwale of the boat and Mott deftly twisted the craft around in a tight arc and pointing it downstream.

Bolan scrambled over the edge and Mott raced down the river.

THREE HUNDRED YARDS downriver Jack Grimaldi waited with rotors turning on the flat-decked, converted garbage barge. Together Bolan and Mott maneuvered the unconscious Lerekhov into the helicopter.

"Benson and Sparks?" Bolan demanded as Grimaldi lifted the helicopter up and raced for the coast.

"Already in Thailand!" Grimaldi shouted. "Nice job, Striker! Hal's going to be ecstatic. The Man took a real personal interest in this one. Those Iranian codes are going to change everything."

Bolan exhaled deeply and collapsed back in his seat. He reached over and grabbed Lerekhov's wrist in his hand, making sure the pulse was present. When he felt it, he grinned and gave the Stony Man pilots a thumb's-up.

"I DON'T NEED TO TELL YOU what a great job you did today, Mack," Hal Brognola said into the video conference camera. "But I'm going to anyway—that was one hell of a stunt you pulled off in Myanmar."

"Nice to be appreciated," Bolan said.

He settled back into the leather seat of the executive jet as Grimaldi raced across the night sky toward a U.S. military outpost in Djibouti. A Special Forces medic and a CIA flight nurse were in the rear of the passenger compartment with the sleeping Lerekhov, monitoring the President's latest acquisition in the war on global terror.

"Yes, it is," Brognola said. "The Man thinks so, too. He wants to thank you personally."

"I don't know, Hal—" Bolan began.

"I won't hear of it, Mack. You deserve it, he owes it and it can only help Stony Man."

"All right." Bolan relented. He was too tired to argue. "I'll meet with him. When and where?"

"He said as soon as you touch down," Brognola said. "He doesn't care what he's doing or what time it is, he wants to thank you personally. Those Lerekhov written codes for the Iranians are critical, but a personal thank-you like this has been a long time coming. You'll probably ride in a secure limo with him for ten minutes, then he'll go make a speech and you can catch some much needed R&R."

"Sounds like a plan," Bolan agreed.

23

Caine stayed in Washington and stalked the President like an enthusiastic fan. He watched the news, read the Web sites, learned to know the players on the scene from the safety of his television and the public library computer screens. The country was at war, threats were real: 9/11 had proved that. Of course that truth had resulted in one hell of a blank check.

He caught his chance more quickly than he could have dared hope when it was announced that the President would attend a high-profile function at the Holocaust Memorial Museum. For a brief moment the building horror of the Iranian confrontation took a backseat.

The United States Holocaust Memorial Museum sat on the east side of the intersection of Independence Avenue and Fourteenth Street. Caine knew from his research that the Washington D.C. Police Department would erect a security cordon around the area, directing traffic. Secret Service countersniper teams would deploy on rooftops and bomb-sniffing dogs would patrol the street in random sweeps.

On the day of the function Caine put the Buick Skylark into position first. He waited with patience of the hunter for the spot at the intersection of Independence and Fifteenth Street. He backed into the spot so that his trunk was pointed due west, out toward the traffic on Fifteenth Street.

He got out of the car dressed in upscale casual clothing like a lobbyist on his day off. He had sealed the Astrolite A into plastic gallon bags inside the bins, including one with the cell-phone detonator. Over this he had packed in fire-retardant foam from commercial extinguishers, an old drug smuggler's trick to neutralize scent.

He knew the plan wasn't perfect. Perfect was for theoretical worlds. In the land where people got dirty, risk factors could be reduced but never eliminated. There was risk involved. It wasn't like writing opinionated political drivel on an Internet blog; it was getting the deed done.

He left the car and went to place the van.

He parked the twelve-seat Dodge van in one of the lanes specially designated for those commercial enterprises on Fifteenth Street at the point where Independence Avenue divided Fifteenth Street from 100 Raoul Wallenberg Place. He had constructed a tight kill box. To the north the Washington Monument thrust upward like a finger into the sky.

He got out of the tour van wearing generic blue coveralls and a Washington Redskins baseball cap while he placed his Maintenance placards, fore and aft of the van, warning the other tour crews of his mechanical problems. He did this very late, toward the end of the business day, as local tours stopped running at 3:00 p.m., but well before the Holocaust gala was scheduled to begin.

He used the public rest rooms near the Washington Monument to strip out of his cap and coveralls. While he changed into his street clothes and stuffed his disguise in a black nylon gym bag, he reviewed his plan.

As he walked across to the National Mall to where he'd left the Suburban, he whistled "It'll Be a Hot Time in the Old Town Tonight" and he felt pretty damn good.

As PROMISED, Brognola had arranged for Bolan to accompany the President in his limousine on the way to the Holocaust memorial. The Man had insisted that only a personal thank-you could adequately express his appreciation for the success of Bolan's most recent overseas mission.

"Without your assistance, threats on foreign soil and here at home would be looming large," the President told Bolan.

"Thank you, sir," Bolan said.

Though they were traveling inside a bulletproof limousine in the middle of a highly secure presidential motorcade, Bolan hadn't relaxed his vigilance. He was scanning the crowd of spectators that lined the streets, eager for a glimpse of the President. The Executioner couldn't help thinking that regardless of his recent success, danger was never nearer than now. His battle senses were on high alert, and despite being surrounded by the presidential security detail, he couldn't escape the feeling of an approaching threat.

CAINE HAD STACKED his drugs like his body armor, each pill working like the snip of the scissors, cutting him off from his past, from himself, from any hope of a future. His mission was deeply personal, the way the most important missions always were, but it was about more than him, more than revenge.

Official mantles had a way of insulating their holders from the consequences of their actions. A government official couldn't be sued for actions taken in the course of his or her duties. The government didn't offer the right of litigation against itself. Individuals made decisions that affected millions on deeply personal levels and then fled to ivy-covered citadels protected by protocol and legalese.

A government should be afraid of its people, not a people afraid of its government.

He sat in the blacked-out Suburban and watched the Capitol police block off the side streets as the presidential procession rolled through. From his vantage Caine could see the front of the Holocaust procession. He made no moves that would alert the Secret Service countersniper marksmen.

Out of respect for their capabilities he had combined each of his vehicle-based improvised-explosive devices with hundred-pound smoke bombs. The resulting smoke on top of that from the primary explosions would saturate the area around the blasts with thick, choking smoke. Visibility would be obscured at close range. Rooftop snipers would be useless.

He wore body armor rated up to .30-caliber weapons. The ceramic and titanium plate inserts would negate most long guns for at least a couple of shots. The Secret Service was armed with Beretta pistols and H&K MP-5 submachine guns, both chambered in 9 mm. His Kevlar weave alone would reduce their impact to the point of negation.

It would hurt each time he was hit, but that was what the drugs were for.

Caine recalled the December 1997 robbery of the Bank of America branch on Laurel Canyon Boulevard in North Hollywood. The resulting shootout with police had changed the face of American law enforcement. Only the lesson, much like the Columbine massacre, had not been universal and not every law-enforcement agency in the country had learned it.

The two Bank of America robbers had been armed with main battle rifles, heavy body armor and their systems flooded with barbiturates, making them impervious to pain, shock or the effects of panic. They had walked through hails of 9 mm police gunfire, their body armor protecting them from the majority of wounds, the barbiturates allowing them to simply ignore the rest. The bank robbers had used their own Kalashnikov assault rifles to blast apart police vehicles, penetrate officer body armor and suppress platoons of law-enforcement agents.

They couldn't be stopped. One had committed suicide in the middle of the street. The second had finally been taken out by leg and head shots at nearly point-blank range only after dealing out a horrendous amount of damage.

Caine intended to do them better. Always in good physical condition, the weight of his body armor was hardly a burden. He had begun gobbling Oxycotin. The popular painkiller produced not only incredible analgesic capabilities, but also provided a powerful but calm euphoria. Caine was physiologically incapable of panic.

When the drug began to make him woozy, he snorted crank until his brain buzzed like high-voltage wires and he felt as if he could fly. As the presidential motorcade rolled past to attend the Holocaust gala, Caine began placing drops under his tongue designed to keep female dogs from going into heat. In humans the fast-acting anabolic hormone caused extreme levels of aggression and, when mixed with methamphetamine, Caine had efficiently changed his biological makeup into that of a homicidally enraged sociopath.

Better killing through modern chemistry, he thought.

To his main vest Caine had added both sleeve and waist-bib blast-protection attachments designed for bomb-squad personnel. He wore steel-toed boots with tough rubber soles and the same shin guards and hockey masks utilized by riot police. Over the black face mask he wore a Kevlar helmet with a face shield. Designed to fit law-enforcement and military helmets, the shield featured integral rubber seals to provide a liquid barrier at the helmet-shield interface.

As the night deepened, he felt increasingly powerful, invulnerable. Like Darth Vader or a Storm Trooper commando, he thought, impersonal. He listened to a classic rock station with his AKM resting across his lap like an obedient dog while he worked at the folds of the government letter in his hand like a string of prayer beads. He sang along to songs on the oldies station, trying to keep a lid on his rage. He didn't think about anything but the skyline above the Potomac.

He felt the rising power welling in him in an emotional volcano as he sat behind his blacked-out windows and waited for his chance. People had begun to gather outside the Holocaust Memorial waiting for the President to exit his vehicle.

Caine wore pistols under either arm and on each thigh. He slid the sling of the Kalashnikov around his neck and checked the seat of his 200-round drum magazine. He had a skeletonized boot knife hanging upside down from his dual pistol harness. He reached over and opened the glove box, pulled an ice pick out and stuck it deep in the passenger's seat.

He hit the power button on his CD player and keyed up his copy of Metallica's *Kill 'Em All* album. The uncompromising riffs at the beginning of "Seek & Destroy" filled the cab, and Caine's eyes narrowed like a cat's in pleasure. He felt his heart begin to pound in his chest, and goose bumps rose as adrenaline flooded his system. He felt good, felt alive and he wasn't thinking about Charisa or Emma or the old man alone in that trailer park, or about Justin who'd been sold out to politics in a desert nation halfway around the world. He patted the folded paper of the government letter.

Caine picked up his cell phone and prepped his speed dial. He eased the big black Suburban, identical in almost every way to the ones interspersed among the limousines of the fast approaching motorcade, out into the street. Up ahead on Independence Avenue a black-and-white patrol car blocked off traffic. Two officers stood on the street to either side of their vehicle.

It was evening, well past rush hour, and the traffic on Independence was light. To make his approach at good speed, Caine needed to cross the center and race up the other lane.

One of the police officers stood at the open passenger's-side door, talking into his radio. Parked at the intersection only yards away sat Caine's vehicle-based IED. Just as Caine reached the first of the civilian cars lined up by the police roadblock, the first vehicle of the presidential motorcade zipped past, lights flashing and siren wailing.

Caine wheeled the Suburban into the wrong lane and watched the mix of black limos and giant SUVs race past his point. The police officer on his radio saw the behemoth Chevy Suburban break ranks and he stepped away from his car. With the tint on the windows the big vehicle looked official.

Momentarily confused, the officer turned to look back at the convoy running up Fourteenth Street behind him, obviously wondering if the Suburban belonged to the press corps or the Secret Service.

"Number nine," Caine said and he wouldn't have recognized his own voice if he could have heard it from beneath his hockey mask.

He hit the speed dial and the explosion came hard half a heartbeat later. The explosion was rolling thunder as the tour van just north of his position blew. The boom was so loud glass shattered up and down the stretch of street and a volcanic column of pitch black rose into the air. Secondary explosions of vehicle gas tanks rupturing tripped in daisy-cutter chains, and metal pieces from ripped-apart automobiles began raining down.

It was on.

24

Immediately after the explosion there was a squeal of brakes as impeccably trained Secret Service drivers began reacting. A burning body arced out of the smoke and bounced hard off the pavement. The windshield had been blown out of the limo, and Caine caught a glimpse of two charred corpses flopping like dolls.

One-handed, Caine guided the Suburban fully into the empty street lane on Independence Avenue. The two policemen at the intersection had been tossed to the ground and a three-foot-long piece of fender jutted from their windshield like the hilt of a sword.

More chemical machine than human, Caine used his thumb to queue up his speed dial. In the middle of the street Secret Service drivers were already beginning to execute their evasive maneuvers. The downed policeman closer to Caine pushed himself up off the street, hands scrambling for his gun.

The trunk of the Buick Skylark exploded with devastating, merciless force. More black-and-white smoke rolled out across the street like a supernatural sea fog, and the entire intersection was immediately obscured. The police cruiser and two civilian cars parked behind it at the checkpoint were thrown onto their sides like playing cards and their gas tanks erupted in orange flames.

Caine couldn't hear the screams as he gunned the Suburban

forward. All he could hear was the roar of the Suburban's big-block engine as he gunned it directly toward the smoke and violent turmoil.

BOLAN SPOTTED THE BLACK Suburban charging up through the smoke that followed the initial explosion, and he knew that more mayhem would surely follow. It was his job to limit the damage, protect the President and his wife as best he could.

"Get down," he instructed the President and the first lady.

The Executioner moved across the rear compartment to place himself between the President and the onrushing Suburban. He knew they were safer inside the vehicle than trying to make a run for safety, but still he felt helpless.

The flash of the second detonation blinded Bolan, and in the moment before the concussive wave rocked the limousine, he threw himself forward to shield the President. Then he was flung back against the seat, and his world went black and silent.

THE SUBURBAN SHUDDERED as he rolled over the charred corpse of one of the D.C. cops. Caine cut around the funeral pyre of one vehicle and launched himself into the smoke.

Car number nine contained the rapid-reaction force of SWAT officers, which was the reason Caine had targeted that vehicle specifically. The SWAT team would be armed with 5.56 mm M-4 carbines and their armor would be more advanced than that of the rank-and-file VIP protection agents. Caine had seen the Skylark-trunk blast push the SWAT SUV over onto its side, and he felt sure he had bought himself long, precious moments.

The trouble was the President. Generally the President rode in vehicle number six, but in reality it could be cars five, six or seven if the Secret Service used a shell-game strategy.

Caine's plan for picking out the President was simple. He'd watch to see which vehicle the agents and officers scrambled to protect, and he would rain hell down on that one.

Out of the smoke a crumpled, stalled limousine appeared. Vehicle number seven. Caine cut the wheel to the side to avoid the wreck. A uniformed police officer with a 12-gauge shotgun appeared suddenly in the middle of the street. The bumper of the Suburban slapped the man hard and sent him tumbling away like a bowling pin.

An eddy in the smoke showed a limo turned diagonally in the street—all the rubber on its tires had been blown clean of the wheels. Instinct made Caine home in on the vehicle. He had captured the line of vehicles like a digital snapshot in his mind before triggering the first blast, and he was absolutely sure he was running down vehicle number six, the designated presidential limousine.

As he surged forward, the limo's door popped open and a wild-looking man in a dark suit scrambled out. A flat, black automatic pistol filled his hand and his dazed expression twisted into startled fear and anger as he saw Caine's Suburban racing toward him.

The agent lifted his Beretta and began pumping rounds at the monster SUV as it ran him down. He made no attempt to save his own life, and Caine's suspicions about the position of the President were confirmed. The 9 mm rounds pinged and whined as they ricocheted off the engine block, but Caine was doing close to forty miles per hour by the time he hit and nothing was going to slow him down.

The front of the Suburban SUV slammed into the body-guard, pinning him between vehicle grille and the limo door. The man screamed hard as blood painted the Suburban's windshield in the brief moment before the air bag deployed.

Caine felt the reverberation of the impact travel up through the steering column and shake him like a child.

Though braced for the impact, he was still jerked forward violently. The exploding air bag burst out and slammed him backward with stunning force. The concussion rattled him, but because of his chemical cocktail Caine was at once too relaxed and too keyed up to be subdued.

His searching hand found the handle of the ice pick where it thrust up from the cushion of the passenger's seat. He wrapped his fingers around it in a tight fist and yanked it free before plunging it into the side of the air bag pinning him to the seat. The deflation was instantaneous, and he felt air rushing out as the bag collapsed under him like a punctured lung.

Moving fast, he threw open the driver's door even as multiple car alarms began blaring around him. The strap of his AKM pulled against his neck as he backed out of the vehicle, dragging the ballistic shield out of the Suburban cab along with him.

He hit the ground and the smoke choked him immediately. The glassy eyes of the dead agent looked at Caine from the crumpled, bloody hood of his vehicle. He heard angry shouts, knew desperate men were running closer now. He banked on his quasiofficial appearance slowing the approaching agents' reaction times and granting him initiative.

Confusion reigned on the scene. He looked like one of the good guys, and the explosions could have caused the Suburban-versus-limousine wreck. He had a number of situational factors he was exploiting to shift and keep momentum. The ballistic shield was up and on his arm. He held the Kalashnikov by its pistol grip and pushed out against the tension of the sling strapped around his body, forming a fulcrum that worked as a third hand.

Caine stepped around the open door of his SUV. He was close enough to rake the inside of the limo with his Kalashnikov. He sensed movement and whirled, instinctively bringing up the shield. He was so chemically jacked his slightest motion rewarded him with nearly preternatural results.

The Secret Service agents raced out of the roiling smoke, their hands raised protectively over faces as they cried toxins clear of their eyes, Beretta pistols naked in their fists. They saw Caine, suited up like a riot cop but then registered the incongruous shape of his drum-mounted AKM assault rifle.

Caine scythed them down in a wild, loose Z-pattern burst designed to take them in the low belly, groin and hips beneath the protection of their body armor. Screaming, the agents fell, blood spurting from their wounds. One of the agents, a beefy man with a blond crew cut, managed to get off two tight shots despite his crippling pain, but the 9 mm pistol rounds struck the ballistic shield and Caine finished him off with a 5-round burst that tore the crew cut off his head.

Caine spun back toward the presidential limo and saw an agent drawing down across the roof of the vehicle above the middle-compartment doors. Caine ducked behind the ballistic shield and the pistol round careened off the top of his Kevlar helmet, staggering him.

He fired a burst of the heavy 7.62 mm slugs. The recoil shook the weapon in his hand, sending reverberations up his arm like an industrial jackhammer. The softball-size lump of his bicep knotted in reaction to the stress but held the bucking weapon easily. Shell casings spilled out of the oversize ejection port in a tumbling arc of spinning brass to bounce off the black asphalt at his feet. Cordite fumes filled his nose with the stink of burned gunpowder, invigorating him.

Caine had loaded his drum with a tracer every third round

to help him direct his aim while he fired one-handed. A laserlike stream of bullets poured into the immobilized limousine. It shattered the bullet-resistant glass like falling hammers and ripped through the cavity between the car doors. A tracer round, burning lava hot, burrowed into the seat stuffing under the plush leather seats and set the bench on fire.

Three more rifle rounds struck the firing Secret Service agent, shattering his femurs and kneecaps. The man shrieked in agonized shock and spun away from the limo, dropping to the street. Kane stepped out to the side and pivoted so that the smoking muzzle of his Kalashnikov was aimed through the shattered window and toward the interior of the presidential vehicle. He saw the pitch-black glass divider separating the rear compartment of the limo from the center and aimed his fire toward it.

He triggered a burst and cackled in glee as the glass divider spiderwebbed under the impact of his fusillade. The driver's door flew open to his left, and Caine turned, hidden behind the shield on his arm.

The driver, his face black-eyed and bruised from his own air bag deployment, was still dazed by the impact of Caine's Suburban but managed to throw himself from the car, sweeping up the Beretta in his hands. Caine dropped into a crouch behind the ballistic shield as the pistol roared. The bullets snapped into the shield, shoving it hard up against Caine's Kevlar-protected shoulder and arm.

He was slow turning in the bulky armor with his long weapon and some distant, disembodied part of his mind thought a collapsible-stock weapon would have been more versatile even as he closed the distance. It didn't matter, he thought just as dispassionately, there were no do-overs. The Secret Service agent burned through his magazine trying to bring Caine down, but the assassin was impervious to the bullets.

Caine brought the Kalashnikov to bear and burned off a burst from point-blank range, splashing blood from the government bodyguard across the street. Caine rose as the agent riding shotgun dived across the front seats and fired.

Sparks shot off the street as the man aimed for Caine's ankles in an attempt to bring him down. A 9 mm Parabellum round ricocheted up and shattered the ceramic insert on Caine's shin guards. Caine staggered, almost tripping, and three pistol rounds struck him center mass in the back, failing to crack the titanium plates secured in his vest's Kevlar weave. The kinetic energy staggered him, but the pain impulse from the blunt-force trauma never reached his brain.

Caine threw his arm out to block the rounds coming in from the side and raised the red-hot muzzle of the AKM. The agent in the limo front seat fired twice, catching him high on the torso, but the rounds were ineffective for anything besides staggering Caine back into the door of his Suburban.

Caine triggered the AKM, screaming as he rained fire down on the man without remorse. Blood splattered the inside windshield of the limousine, and the agent's body shuddered. With the trigger still held down, Caine swept his weapon around as he spun toward his other attackers.

A pistol round cleared the lip of the shield and slammed into his Kevlar helmet, cracking the ballistic face shield at an attachment point. Caine's head snapped back under the concussive impact and his ankle, weakened by the pistol round that had cracked his shin guard, turned, spilling him to the ground.

From his back Caine fired his AKM, jerking the muzzle in a careless figure-eight pattern that threw out a virtual wall of lead across the width of Fourteenth Street. He saw government agents jerk and dance as his main battlefield rounds burrowed into them, easily knifing through their own lighter ballistic vests. They hit the ground hard under the onslaught and flopped like fish cast into the bottom of a boat.

Out of the smoke a SWAT member, dragging a bleeding and nearly useless leg, appeared. He wore a Kevlar helmet and heavy vest. In his hands was a 5.56 mm M-4 carbine. The collapsible stock was extended and the trooper shuffled forward in ungraceful movements, firing 3-round bursts in tight, precise patterns.

The bursts struck the downed Caine, shattering his inserts under the impact of the high-velocity rounds. Caine drew into a fetal position under his shield, gasping for breath as deep bruises mottled on his body under his armor. He lifted the Kalashnikov and cut the SWAT team gunner off at the knees.

The man screamed long and loud as he fell, his head bouncing mightily off the street. Caine met his eyes across the scant twenty yards and saw the bodyguard's pain and terror.

Was that how Justin had looked when they got him? Caine wondered as he pulled the trigger on his AKM and finished off the helpless agent.

Shaken and hurt from dozens of impact injuries, Caine forced himself to his feet. He felt short of breath but not tired, not by a long shot. A stray bullet had sliced the sling of the Kalashnikov and he left the assault rifle lying forgotten on the smoking, bloodstained street. Agents fired from across the hood of the closest vehicle, but again the pistol rounds proved ineffective against Caine's ballistic shield.

His hand went to the big handgun on his right thigh. He closed a possessive fist around the pistol grip of his Automag V .50-caliber pistol. He yanked the massive handgun clear of its nylon shoulder holster as multiple rounds ricocheted off the Suburban and the limousine around him. Caine leveled the clumsy hand cannon.

Reinforcements from the police and Secret Service began arriving on the scene, looking panicked and brandishing weapons. The law-enforcement officials were frantic and nearly suicidal in their attempts to reach the President's vehicle. Caine threw himself forward into the bloody seat of the limousine's middle compartment.

Bits of flesh like scraps of torn wet paper were splashed across the interior, mixed with chunks of pink matter and enough blood to fill a children's wading pool. The ballistic shield couldn't fit through the door opening, and Caine's dive was jerked short. Rounds struck the shield like lead raindrops as he fought to free his arm.

Because the ballistic shield was attached to his left arm, Caine found himself in an awkward position, sprawled out across the smoldering midcompartment seat with his back toward the rear. He would be forced to fire over his gun hand shoulder toward his own back unless he could free himself from the shield. Across the seat he could see out through the open door into a wall of black smoke.

The glass divider into the rear compartment was spiderwebbed across its length with impact damage and Caine raised the heavy pistol, firing from centimeters away. Muzzleflash spit from the barrel like flame from a dragon's mouth. The big handgun bucked hard in Caine's grip, and the report was loud enough to hurt even Caine's explosion-deafened ears. The angle of his grip on the pistol was so awkward the recoil almost ripped the heavy Automag from his fingers.

A hole the size of a golf ball punched through the already compromised safety glass. Caine heard a high-pitched shriek of terror. He went to trigger the .50-caliber hand cannon again.

Out on his right side, through the open limo door, he caught the flash of movement. The rear-compartment passenger's door flew open and Caine knew his prey was trying to escape.

Suddenly he was jerked from the left. A man in a dark suit grabbed the edge of his ballistic shield where it was caught in the door, desperately trying to pry it back. A uniformed officer with a Glock pistol shoved his handgun around the edge and began to fire into the limo.

The range was brutally close and 9 mm bullets hammered into Caine like clubs. He groaned out loud under their savage impact. A bullet smashed through the face shield and then shattered the hard plastic of the black hockey mask.

Caine's cheekbone cracked under the concussive force and jagged splinters of plastic lanced his eye, blinding him. He bucked as though electrocuted and screamed, the Automag falling from his hands. He felt slugs strike him in the already shattered inserts over his abdomen. He was too weak to fight, and the agent hanging on to his shield managed to straighten his arm all the way out at the elbow.

Caine brought his right hand up. A 9 mm slug blew his pinkie off, but the wound seemed so distant to his shocked mind it was almost as if it had occurred to someone else's body. His wounded hand reached the suspender strap of his harness where he had secured the garage-door opener with black electrician's tape.

His finger found the rectangular activation button and pressed it.

There was peace.

Gravity was gone and silence held Caine in a vacuum cocoon. He felt the world turn in a slow somersault, like a carnival ride. Justin had loved the carnival when they were kids, but the second-rate affairs the old man had been able to take them to had quickly killed the charm for Caine.

Justin never seemed to see past the neon and the primary colors to feel the grit of the dust or see the grime or the toothless, hollow-eyed smiles of the operators and barkers. He believed in the magic even after he grew old enough not to. For all Caine knew, Justin had believed right up until the Iraqi police unit had come under fire at the roadside checkpoint and left the Marines on their own.

Maybe Justin had never stopped believing the way Caine had after Mogadishu. Maybe he kept right on believing while the 7.62 mm AKM rounds had chewed into his body from that unprotected flank. The government letter, the followup to the official visit, hadn't touched on that part. It hadn't mentioned what the An Bar insurgents had done to Justin's body after the ambush, either. But Justin had been stubborn, just like their old man had taught them, and maybe he'd gone right on believing.

In a way, Caine kind of hoped so.

The spinning limousine hit the ground with a shudder and Caine's forearm snapped inside the shield braces with a clean, audible crack. His body was tossed around like a bull rider's inside the limo cab. The big black vehicle tottered on its side for a moment, then pitched over onto the roof.

The ceiling caved in and the compromised safety glass divider shattered further, ripping like cloth. Caine lay twisted and bruised, his mind stunned but his body so supercharged on methamphetamine that he was hardly slowed at all. He had lost the Automag when he'd detonated the charge in the trunk of the Suburban. Waves of heat poured off the burning vehicle, and through his shield Caine got the impression of a massive crater in the middle of the street.

He slid his broken left arm out from the shield braces. He felt something wet and heavy tangled up in the broken face shield of his helmet and he used his right hand to slap at it. A human jawbone, looking like a crimson boomerang, fell away as he knocked it aside.

Caine was deaf as he pulled himself up. Like the persistent ringing of a telephone, the pain from his body kept trying to draw his attention but the warm gauze of his Oxycotin high made it easy to ignore. He could see through the dangling shreds of the ruined safety glass into the rear compartment of the limousine.

He saw a big, black-haired man in a black bodysuit lying unconscious on the floor. A middle-aged woman in an expensive evening dress lay unconscious across a gray-haired man in a blood-splattered tuxedo. Scarlet leaked from the man's slack mouth and her eardrum. The man looked up, blinking confusion from pained eyes. The President.

Caine snarled and drew his knife. His rage was primal and senseless, and maybe if he hadn't been so high he would have drawn one of his remaining pistols, but his target was close and it revved his bloodlust beyond his ability for reason.

Caine slid the boot knife from its sheath and lunged forward, but his armor-bulked shoulders caught in the narrow window opening.

The President roused out of his stupor and saw the ruined, bloody face of his assassin come snarling straight at him. The most powerful man in the world threw himself across the inert form of his comatose wife, trying desperately to protect her. Caine shoved himself through the opening, swinging the fighting knife like a lion's claw. The door on the President's left side popped open. Caine had an impression of a forest of legs and feet crowding around the opening. Waves of heat from Caine's burning Suburban washed into the ruined limo compartment like hellish wind.

Caine tried to grab the lapels of the President's jacket, but his left arm was broken and he couldn't make his hand move properly. With only one eye working he could no longer gauge his depth perception, and when he slashed again, his knife missed the inviting target. Instead he sank three inches of stainless steel deep into a Secret Service agent's shoulder.

"The blood of martyrs," Caine whispered, unaware he'd spoken.

Blood splashed and Caine struck again, trying to fight off the bodyguard. The diving agent's momentum wrenched the fighting knife out of Caine's grasp and instinctively he went for the pistol slung under his left shoulder.

Strong hands grasped him by his straining legs and yanked hard. He turned onto his side to kick free and clear the weapon from its shoulder holster. He saw a square-jawed black man, his face streaked with soot, thrust himself over the agent who had taken the knife to the shoulder.

Caine thought about the twenty-foot aluminum Boston Whaler with the twin outboards waiting for him in the Potomac Tidal Basin just off Independence Avenue. It's time to go, he thought. Better get home now, got to see Charisa and Emma. They're probably worried.

Caine felt the muzzle of the Secret Service agent's pistol strike him hard under the chin, forcing his head back painfully. Instinctively Caine pulled the trigger on the Ruger P-95 he was drawing even though he hadn't cleared the holster yet.

He felt suddenly tired as the gun flashed hot under his arm and he put a 10 mm bullet through the wing of his own *latissimus dorsi* muscle. He looked in the direction of the pain with his good eye and registered the Secret Service agent's arm and the hard metal press of the gun muzzle under his chin. He killed the black Secret Service agent.

MACK BOLAN SWAM UP out of unconsciousness as the last agent died. He was moving before his mind had fully articulated the chaos swirling around him. His hand found the trigger of the agent's pistol still shoved up against the bloody attempted assassin, whose eyes were squeezed shut.

Bolan yanked the trigger, and the assassin's head exploded.

Bolan quickly dropped the smoking pistol, his head still spinning, to prevent confused Secret Service agents from firing on him. He looked at the ruined, gunshot deformed head of the assassin and let his breath escape.

He turned toward the President as more Secret Service agents pushed their way into the car.

"Are you two okay, sir?" he asked.

The President looked at the first lady, then nodded to Bolan. "I think so."

Moving slowly so as not to panic the keyed-up security team, Bolan pulled out his cell phone to call Hal Brognola, who was riding in a SUV well behind the main motorcade. He was going to need a ride out of here before the media cameras arrived in force.

He had traveled all this way just to shoot a would-be presidential assassin at point-blank range. Even for me, he thought as he dialed Brognola's number, this is strange.

The irony was not lost on the Executioner. Moments earlier he had received a personal thank-you from the President, and he had no doubt that another would soon be forthcoming.

Don Pendleton
DRAWPOINT

American politics have been infiltrated by terrorist
elements, and they're ready to launch something
big involving radical environmentalists, wealthy
businessmen and a political insider. With time
running out, Stony Man races to stop an enemy
armed with stolen uranium from unleashing a
shock wave of violence to hijack the White House
and the American way of life.

STONY
MAN®

*Available June 2009
wherever books are sold.*

Or order your copy now by sending your name, address, zip or postal code, along with a check or
money order (please do not send cash) for $6.99 for each book ordered ($7.99 in Canada), plus
75¢ postage and handling ($1.00 in Canada), payable to Gold Eagle Books, to:

In the U.S.	In Canada
Gold Eagle Books	Gold Eagle Books
3010 Walden Avenue	P.O. Box 636
P.O. Box 9077	Fort Erie, Ontario
Buffalo, NY 14269-9077	L2A 5X3

Please specify book title with your order.
Canadian residents add applicable federal and provincial taxes.

**GOLD
EAGLE**®

www.readgoldeagle.blogspot.com

GSM101

TAKE 'EM FREE

2 action-packed novels plus a mystery bonus

NO RISK

NO OBLIGATION TO BUY

SPECIAL LIMITED-TIME OFFER

Mail to: Gold Eagle Reader Service

IN U.S.A.: P.O. Box 1867, Buffalo, NY 14240-1867
IN CANADA: P.O. Box 609, Fort Erie, Ontario L2A 5X3

YEAH! Rush me 2 FREE Gold Eagle® novels and my FREE mystery bonus (bonus is worth about $5). If I don't cancel, I will receive 6 hot-off-the-press novels every other month. Bill me at the low price of just $31.94 for each shipment.* That's a savings of over 15% off the combined cover prices and there is NO extra charge for shipping and handling! There is no minimum number of books I must buy. I can always cancel at any time simply by returning a shipment at your cost or by returning any shipping statement marked "cancel." Even if I never buy another book from Gold Eagle, the 2 free books and mystery bonus are mine to keep forever.

166 ADN EF29 366 ADN EF3A

Name	(PLEASE PRINT)
Address	Apt. #
City	State/Prov.	Zip/Postal Code

Signature (if under 18, parent or guardian must sign)

Not valid to current subscribers of Gold Eagle books.
Want to try two free books from another series? Call 1-800-873-8635.

* Terms and prices subject to change without notice. N.Y. residents add applicable sales tax. Canadian residents will be charged applicable provincial taxes and GST. Offer not valid in Quebec. This offer is limited to one order per household. All orders subject to approval. Credit or debit balances in a customer's account(s) may be offset by any other outstanding balance owed by or to the customer. Please allow 4 to 6 weeks for delivery. Offer available while quantities last.

Your Privacy: Worldwide Library is committed to protecting your privacy. Our Privacy Policy is available online at www.eHarlequin.com or upon request from the Reader Service. From time to time we make our lists of customers available to reputable third parties who may have a product or service of interest to you. If you would prefer we not share your name and address, please check here.

GE08R

Don Pendleton's Mack Bolan®

Interception

The city of Split, Croatia, is a multinational den of thieves, where conspiracy, corruption and criminal cells rival for profit and power. Mack Bolan is on its violent streets, trying to stop the global traffickers from doing what they do best—selling death. Fully aware of the mounting odds on all fronts, Bolan is betting on surviving this mission. Again.

Available May 2009
wherever books are sold.

Or order your copy now by sending your name, address, zip or postal code, along with a check or money order (please do not send cash) for $6.99 for each book ordered ($7.99 in Canada), plus 75¢ postage and handling ($1.00 in Canada), payable to Gold Eagle Books, to:

In the U.S.	In Canada
Gold Eagle Books	Gold Eagle Books
3010 Walden Avenue	P.O. Box 636
P.O. Box 9077	Fort Erie, Ontario
Buffalo, NY 14269-9077	L2A 5X3

GOLD EAGLE®

Please specify book title with your order.
Canadian residents add applicable federal and provincial taxes.

www.readgoldeagle.blogspot.com

GSB126

AleX Archer
SACRIFICE

On assignment in the Philippines, archaeologist
Annja Creed meets with a contact to verify
some information. But when the man doesn't
turn out to be who he said he was, Annja
finds herself a prisoner of a
notorious terrorist group.
Though she manages to
escape, Annja is soon
struggling to stay alive
amidst terrorists and not-
so-dead jungle spirits with
a taste for human flesh.

**Available May 2009
wherever books are sold.**

www.readgoldeagle.blogspot.com

GRA18